TO THE
GREEN
VALLEYS
YONDER

A WESTERN FRONTIER ADVENTURE

ROBERT PEECHER

For information the author may be contacted at PO Box 967; Watkinsville GA; 30677

or at rob@mooncalfpress.com

This is a work of fiction. Any similarities to actual events in whole or in part are purely accidental. None of the characters or events depicted in this novel are intended to represent actual people.

ISBN – 9798858201458

CONTENTS

1

OLD GABE BRIDGER RESEMBLED a skeleton, his head like a skull with a thick beard, his skin so drawn and no flesh on his bones. Still, a man couldn't deny the sinewy strength in his arms. He never sat still much, always busy.

Elias Townes watched him move from one camp to another outside the famous fort known to all travelers west. His name was Jim Bridger. Somewhere along the way folks had taken to calling him Old Gabe. In the summer of 1846, he was pushing the stragglers still at his fort to get moving. He said he wanted them gone for their own good, so they didn't get caught in early snows. But Elias figured it was for more selfish purposes that Old Gabe harangued them. They were eating up his supplies. The stocks that would see Jim Bridger and the residents of his fort through the winter.

"He's making enough money off these folks," Zeke Townes replied to his older brother. "Not to mention the business he's doing with the Indians."

Only a few days at the fort, and Jim Bridger's side business was evident to the emigrants. Late in the afternoon one day, at dusk when the emigrants were all seeing to their suppers, a small band of Indians rode in from the plains and approached one of the small buildings that made up the fort. They unloaded from their ponies blankets and hides and other items to barter, and they came out with supplies wrapped in old burlap. Though hidden by the burlap, a man didn't have to be particularly intelligent to guess at what it was that Bridger was selling there. These burlap-wrapped packages were suspiciously the same length as a rifle. Bridger was selling guns and powder and ammunition to the local Indian population.

Elias shook his head.

"He can make all the money in the world, but he ain't got nowhere to spend any of it out here. Come February, if he's run out of supplies in the fort, he can't eat gold coins. And I've got a notion his Indian friends won't take pity on him. No, he wants us all gone before he ain't got supplies enough to see himself through the winter."

"Fair enough," Zeke agreed. "I'd like to be off, myself. But we've got to make a decision."

"Indeed," Elias said.

That decision had been weighing on Elias for the last two days, ever since his younger brother and the other stragglers had come limping into Bridger's Fort.

Attacked by bandits and harassed by Shoshone warriors out of the Wind Mountains, Zeke and the others had reached Bridger's Fort by pure miracle. One of the wagons operating on skids for the loss of an axle, now replaced.

But that miracle led to the decision now before Elias.

They'd crossed the Missouri late in the spring. Elias and Zeke and their families traveling together. They'd picked up some other families getting a late start, as often happened. They had a small wagon train. More than forty wagons at the outset, though they'd lost some to go-backers and other mishaps. Now they were down to about thirty-six, including Zeke's repaired wagon. But an incident as they approached South Pass put Elias in the uncomfortable position of having to banish his own brother from the wagon train. A disagreement turned violent, and Zeke killed a man. Most agreed it was in self-defense, justifiable as far as that went, but a few of the women among the train said they would not travel with a killer.

Elias, thinking he was doing right, formed a tribunal. Himself, an army veteran by the name of Captain Walker, and a preacher called Reverend Marsh. Elias, determined to be a fair judge even in his own brother's trial, decided if the captain and the reverend could not agree, he would side with whichever of the two men came down on the side of harshness.

Reverend Marsh elected to have Zeke Townes banished from the wagon train, and Elias saw no choice but to vote with the preacher.

And so it had been.

For four hundred miles – or nearly so – Zeke had traveled alone. But when disaster struck for the stragglers, Zeke had been nearby and saved their lives. Among those lives Zeke saved, Marcus Weiss, the man who'd been the loudest at wanting to see Zeke hanged.

The question now hanging over Elias's head, would his brother's banishment stand as they made their way to Oregon City from Bridger's Fort.

"I feel the weight of responsibility," Elias said. "You can understand that?"

"Sure I can," Zeke said. "These people voted to put you in charge of their lives. They elected you captain of this train to get them whole and healthy to Oregon City."

"It's no small thing having people trust you with their lives," Elias said. "But I didn't ask for that. It's not as if I campaigned to be made responsible. There's others who could lead them just as well. And let them, I say. I think my mind is made up, Zeke. I'm going to tell the others that they can go on however they want, but that I'm throwing in with you. We're taking our wagons and going on our own."

Zeke nodded his head.

"We can manage it," he said. "There's safety in numbers, and more hands to spread the hard work. But I trust you to get us all the way, even if we're fewer in number."

"Obviously, Jason and Maggie will come with us," Elias said, speaking of his daughter and her husband. "Caleb and Jerry, the Tucker brothers and the Page boys. They'll all stick with us."

Zeke chuckled.

"I expect that's right, considering their plan is to work for us in Oregon Territory."

"I think Henry Blair would pitch in with us, too."

"Henry's a good boy," Zeke said.

Henry Blair was their hired guide. He wasn't much of a guide, having only made the journey once as a fur trapper. But that was once more than anyone else in the wagon train. And what Henry had said on the eastern bank of the Missouri River was that he wouldn't accept any responsibility, but he'd offer his knowledge and advice where it was warranted.

"I suppose I could tell them that anyone is welcome to stay with us if they want."

Zeke narrowed his eyes, thinking of all the folks who spoke out against him. Jefferson Pilcher had been on Zeke's side, but Jefferson's wife was adamant she would not travel with Zeke after the incident.

"I'd almost rather go on without them," Zeke said. "Let them make their own way, and we'll make our way, and we can see in Oregon City who fares the best."

"Yep," Elias said. "I can see how you'd feel that way. But I guess I'd rather give them the choice. Tell these folks that the Townes Party is going, and anyone who wants to join it is welcome with the understanding that the Townes Party includes all the Towneses."

"Most of 'em have probably figured that out by now," Zeke said.

"Also, Neil Rimmer and his outfit will be with us," Elias said. "I've talked it over with him, and he's committed to going the full way with us. Truthfully, we'd be better off without the rest of the wagon train. We've got a better balance between hands and women and children. We'd probably be able to move faster without them."

"Then don't give them the choice," Zeke suggested with a grin, knowing his brother couldn't bring himself to do such a thing.

And, indeed, Elias Townes shook his head.

"No, sir. I can't just abandon these people. But I can set terms, and this is the place to do it. They can come with us, fully understanding that come what may, you and I travel together. They can go it on their own. Maybe find a guide from among the people here at Bridger's. Or they can winter at the fort and buy in with any one of a hundred wagon trains passing through come spring."

Zeke started to say something. Something about his hard feelings for the others who cast him out, forced him to separate in the wide open wilderness from his wife and child, from his brother. Hard, bitter feelings.

But the something Zeke was going to say stopped short when a boy came running up from the trees down by a creek just west of the fort.

"Mr. Townes!" the boy shouted. "Mr. Townes! They said for you to come on quick!"

Elias recognized this as one of the McKinney children. The McKinneys, Solomon and Wiser. Elias wasn't certain which of the two brothers this boy belonged to.

"What is it, son?" Elias said, standing and walking toward him, meeting him at half the distance. "Has there been an accident?"

"No accident," the boy said. "They's fixin' to kill my pa."

Elias turned to look for Zeke and found him at his shoulder. Without a word, both men broken into a run toward the trees down near the creek.

Pa McKinney had been a Presbyterian preacher who read from the Book of Proverbs every morning, and so when his first son was born, he named him Solomon. No one knew if he had second thoughts, doubts about the oldest boy, or if he'd just caught onto a theme and intended to hold to it, but he named his second son Wiser. Solomon and Wiser said there was a third son David and a fourth son Peter. There were some daughters mixed in there with all those boys, and a second wife somewhere, and finally a fifth son whom Pa McKinney called Calvin.

It was Solomon and Wiser who decided to strike out for the western territory of Oregon, bringing with them their families. Solomon had three children, and Wiser two. Solomon was married to Abigail, and Abigail's sister Sophie and her husband Noah Bloom decided to make the trek as well. Noah and Sophie brought along her and Sophie's mother, Betty Carlisle.

They made for a confusing bunch, all of them. All those McKinney children looked just alike, and Solomon and Wiser could have passed for twins. Zeke, whose family was Quaker until his father decided to be Methodist instead, looked at his own older brother, whom he did not think he resembled at all, and decided that Presbyterian traits must be particularly rigid.

When the McKinney boy spoke of murder, Elias and Zeke broke into a run. The boy had trouble keeping up, but that was no matter because Elias saw in a hurry where he was bound.

Down by the creek a small crowd had gathered at the edge of the bank.

Two burly men held Wiser McKinney with his arms twisted behind his back, his hair, shirt, and britches dripping with water. Wiser wore his salt and pepper hair long, down to his shoulders, just about, and it looked like a raggedly old mop head hanging there.

The crowd appeared to be agitated to no end, several of them shouting unintelligibly and apparently at no one in particular.

Elias reached the chaotic scene and paused, seeing that Wiser was in some distress but no immediate danger. Elias had to catch his breath after the sprint. The crowd, with Wiser in tow, had turned from the creek now and were starting back toward the wide yard where the wagon trains encamped outside of Bridger's Fort. The burly men dragging and jerking Wiser along. They were coming directly toward Elias, thirty yards away still, so there was no need to continue to them.

Zeke appeared at his shoulder again.

"What in the hell is happening here?" Zeke asked, frowning at the unexpected situation.

"Your guess is as good as mine," Elias said.

The crowd consisted of maybe half a dozen men, maybe eight. Elias didn't take time to count them. A couple of women and several children filled out their numbers, making them look like a bigger mob than perhaps they were. In addition, the two burly men who grappled with Wiser McKinney.

They were an angry group, and above the tumult, Elias heard one of the men say, "We should hang the thief."

"What's the matter here?" Elias demanded as they approached.

The two big men who had Wiser by the arms, they certainly had seen Elias for the first time. Now that they were closer, Elias could also see that these men wore britches sodden with water. Wiser also lifted his head. He was gulping air and his eyes look frightened.

"We've caught a thief!" a man from the crowd said, and so Elias turned on that one.

"What thief?" Elias demanded.

"This one here!" the man said, pointing a crooked finger at Wiser McKinney.

"What did he steal?" Elias said.

Elias stood erect in front of the group. He was taller by half a head than any of the men among the mob. Zeke, who was also tall, stepped off to one side, just behind Elias. Between the two of them, they made a formidable wall through which the mob would have to pass.

"I saw him around my wagon earlier. And now I'm missing a sack of coins."

Elias looked at Wiser.

"If he took the coins, he'll return them," Elias said. "Did you take the coins, Wiser?"

"I did not!" Wiser said, his voice sounding strong even though his breath still came laboriously.

"Were these men drowning you, Wiser?" Zeke asked, balling his hands into fists.

"Indeed," Wiser said. "Attempting to. These two held me under repeatedly, trying to submerge a confession from me."

"Turn him loose," Zeke said, but the two men holding Wiser only held him all the tighter, and one of them gave Wiser's arm a twist.

"What evidence do you have against him?" Elias said, returning his attention to the first man who spoke up.

"I saw him around my wagon."

"Have you searched him?" Elias said.

"We did. Indeed, we did conduct a search of his person."

"And did your search conclude with the finding of your coins?"

The man clenched his jaw.

"It did not. But that is beside the point. He might have stashed that sack anywhere."

"And did you attempt to elicit a confession from him while you were dunking him into the creek?" Elias asked.

The man nodded his head.

"We asked him what he done with the sack of coins."

"And what did he tell you?" Elias said.

"That he didn't take no coins."

Elias let that statement hang there in the air for a moment, and he gave a glance to Zeke. Zeke did not look at Elias, though. His eyes remained fixed on the two men holding Wiser McKinney.

"What's your name, friend?" Elias asked.

"My name is Thomas Hedden."

"Mr. Hedden, I've traveled some one thousand miles with that man," Elias said. "I know him to be honest and decent, never a sniff of reprobative conduct. Now, as I come up on your angry little group here, I heard someone suggest that Wiser McKinney should be hanged until dead. Was that you that suggested such a thing?"

"It was," Hedden admitted, and he did so a bit abashedly now.

Zeke kept his eyes on the two burly men, but he admired how his brother was bringing this boil down to a simmer. Elias could do that. Always could. It's what made him a competent leader of a wagon train, a good businessman. It didn't hurt, either, that the Townes men were all tall and strong by nature. Back in Paducah, Elias and Zeke together owned a sawmill and timber business. They intended the same when they arrived in Oregon. Elias was the boss of that mill, but he'd been known to pitch in and swing an ax or tote boards or put his back into a felled tree just like any of the rest of the men. Tall, and strong as an ox, folks tended to want to simmer down in front of Elias. The trick Elias had was to give them the opportunity to calm down without humiliating them.

"Why don't you turn Mr. McKinney loose," Elias said. "And then let's talk this over and see if we can come to some sort of resolution?"

"I saw him over by my wagon," Hedden said.

"And maybe he has an explanation for that," Elias said. "He's not going anywhere. There's no reason for these men to keep holding him like that."

"We ain't turning loose no thief," one of the burly men said.

"I can see why you'd feel that way," Elias said. "But for the moment, we don't even know that Mr. McKinney is a thief. All we know is that you've half drowned him and searched him and you have no evidence that he did anything wrong."

"Hedden seen him by his wagon," the burly man said. "That's evidence."

Elias gave a small shrug.

"It's not evidence of theft," Elias said. "Show me some evidence of theft, or turn loose that man."

Zeke had run out of patience for the conversation. He didn't like it that these men held Wiser McKinney in such a way. Weeks of traveling with the man, Zeke liked the McKinney brothers. He found them aptly named. The lessons from Proverbs at their Presbyterian preacher father's knee had taken root. Both men showed wisdom and thoughtfulness, and Zeke had even hoped that when they all settled in the territory, he might find himself neighbors with the McKinney brothers. And these tough men had given Wiser rough treatment, and Zeke knew damned good and well that Wiser hadn't stolen anything.

"It's enough argument," Zeke said. "Take your hands off the man, or I'll remove them for you."

"Ezekiel," Elias said. "Hold what you got, brother. We're not finished talking this through."

"Sure we are," Zeke said.

For a moment, Elias feared the thing might become a melee. One or two of the men in the crowd looked eager for a fight. But Hedden did not, and neither did most of them. But now, even the two big men let Wiser go, and he dropped to the sandy earth. And Elias saw the reason why when he looked back over his shoulder.

Neil Rimmer and a couple of his boys, and Henry Blair and the Page brothers, Cody and William who were both employees at the Townes lumber mill and bound for Oregon Territory to continue that work. Burly men didn't scare them.

The odds much more even, Hedden gave up.

"I'm going to see Bridger," he said. "I'll have justice here."

"That's fine," Elias said.

The crowd, including the two burly men, the women and the children, and the other men, all marched off now for Bridger's Fort.

Zeke stretched out a hand to Wiser and helped him to his feet.

"We've been here too long," Elias said. "What should have been no more than two days has already stretched into three. We leave before dawn. Whoever chooses can come along with us."

"Yep," Zeke said.

MARCUS WEISS SPOKE AT length to the captain of a train bound for California. But Weiss had made up his mind to go to Oregon Territory, even if it meant continuing on with a party of people whom he despised. He also talked to the captain of another wagon train bound for Oregon City, but the price to buy in was more than he was willing to spend.

Elias Townes had offered him a refund of a portion of the money he'd spent to join the Townes Party. Elias himself was taking no money to captain the wagon train, or at least that's what he claimed. Marcus Weiss didn't know if he believed it. But there'd been other expenses – community livestock and supplies, the hands who pitched in and helped, the Blair boy who was serving as the party's guide and adviser. Much of the money was already spent, though Elias said he'd held back some of the pay for the hands and a pittance for supplies, and that was where the refund would come from.

But the small amount Elias was willing to give back did not meet the price to buy into the other train going to Oregon City. The captain of that wagon train refused to even consider allowing Marcus to buy in at half the rate. He claimed the hardest part of the trail lay ahead and that's where he and the other hands would earn their wages. Marcus Weiss could buy in at the same rate that everyone else paid back east of the Missouri River, or he could make his own way.

"We're stuck with the Townes Party," Marcus Weiss grumbled angrily to his wife.

"If they'll allow us to keep on with them," she said.

She dared not rial her husband, but sometimes she was careless with her tongue. He was a provider, Marcus Weiss, but he could also be cruel with her and the children. He had a short temper and he preferred to take it out on those who could not hit back.

"They'll allow us. Elias has already told me that we can go with the party, but that his brother Zeke will be rejoining the wagon train."

"He saved our lives," Luisa Weiss said to her husband.

She was a frail woman. Her pinched face made her appear older than she was. Marcus was much older than she.

She married him because he was from a German family, as she was, and because he was already wealthy. There'd been no tender courtship. The marriage was more a business arrangement than anything else. Luisa needed a husband who would give her children and provide for her. Marcus needed a wife who would keep house for him. Nothing in the arrangement ever spoke of uprooting the family and moving into the wilderness, and she had objected initially.

But now she rather enjoyed the journey. Despite some of the terrible events, Luisa found that she loved the west. The air smelled so clean and pure. The sky went on a far as her imagination could send it. Everything felt so big and glorious. She'd never seen anything like the Great Plains. Her heart had come alive in the west.

"He is the cause of our lives being in jeopardy in the first place," Marcus reminded her. "Had he not killed our driver Butch, we'd have never been behind the main body of the wagon train with the damaged wagon. We'd have never been easy prey for those bandits. We'd have needed no saving if not for Ezekiel Townes."

"They've been decent to us," Luisa said, it was an off-hand remark that she immediately regretted. She'd been working on darning a pair of britches for one of the children, but she looked up now from her work and saw the fury in her husband's face. "I only mean that they've treated us in a civil manner."

That did not ease his anger.

But he dared not hit her. Not here.

That was the true source of Marcus's hatred of Zeke Townes. Before the incident with Butch, Zeke had spoken to Marcus Weiss about laying hands on Luisa. In no uncertain terms, Zeke had made it plain that if Marcus touched his wife again while they shared the trail, Zeke would give Marcus every bit of it back.

Unaccustomed to being spoken to in such a way, and too afraid of Zeke to challenge him, Marcus had controlled himself. He'd not beat on Luisa after that. Not when Zeke was around, anyway.

But the reprieve in the rough treatment she sometimes took from her husband had made Luisa careless and forgetful. She knew better than to tempt his ire.

"He's a meddler," Marcus said, and his tone had a finality to it that caused Luisa to know that she'd tread too far.

Luisa knew women who had it worse than she. And she'd heard of countless more. Some men beat their wives unmercifully, beat them like men. All Marcus ever gave her were slaps. If he did use his fists or a whip, he was sparing with it. Luisa knew enough about the world to accept small blessings.

They sat in camp chairs on the shady side of their wagon. The three small children ran about, playing with some of the other children from the wagon train. Marcus Weiss did not like his children playing tag or hide-and-seek with the children from the other families in the wagon train. He believed they would learn bad manners and bad behavior from those other children. They were, as a body, dirty children and loud, disrespectful and annoying. The thing Marcus Weiss hated most of all, the cross he head to bear, was the necessity of associating with people whom he despised. He'd not be able to make this journey on his own. Safety came in numbers, and success in the ability to divide the labor. Survival came though people who were there to lend aid at the moment of an emergency.

"What are we to do but to continue on with them?" Marcus said, though this question did not invite an answer from his wife, and so she continued with the patching of the britches. If she'd thought before that children could be hard on clothes at home, she'd learned what hard on clothes meant taking three children across the Emigrant Trail.

"Now what is this?" Marcus said, craning his neck to see beyond the wagon. Luisa could not see a thing, from her position, and other than a glance to confirm so, she did not look up from her work.

Marcus Weiss got out of his camp chair and walked to the back of the wagon and watched a small but growing crowd of people. They must have come from one of the other wagon trains, for he did not recognize any of them. Their postures suggested anger and several among them engaged in heated conversation with looks and even pointed fingers at the cluster of wagons around the Weiss wagon.

Weiss wasn't alone in noticing them. Many of the people in his own wagon train stood and watched the passing crowd.

It was too hot in the day to get overly excited, even about an angry mob, so Marcus watched them from a shady spot.

"I wonder what the matter is yonder," he said to Jefferson Pilcher.

"Some hullabaloo," Pilcher said off-handedly.

Marcus curled his lip at Pilcher's flippant response.

Even the Townes brothers hadn't treated Marcus so cruelly since the episode with Zeke Townes as Jefferson Pilcher. It had been Pilcher's wife who most vociferously demanded that Zeke Townes be banished from the wagon train over the killing of Marcus Weiss's driver. Well, second to Weiss himself. Pilcher regretted her insistence, but was not man enough to stand up to his wife. And his guilt he took out on Marcus.

2

NEIL RIMMER WORE HIS beard long and his hair long. His clothes, britches and shirt, were heavily stained with the elements of the earth. He wore a fringed coat made of some skin, deer or elk or moose. Only his hat looked remotely clean, and that's because he'd just recently bought it there in the trading post at Bridger's Fort.

He stood on the lee side of the fort, leaning against the wall of one of the fort's buildings, watching the angry mob.

"He's found that his sack of coins is missing," Norwood said.

"Likely."

The two men had counted out more than a hundred dollars in coins. They'd folded up the sack and buried it beneath a lone cottonwood tree that stood about sixteen hundred feet northeast of Bridger's Fort. The cottonwood grew in a little drywash that probably only ran with water once every couple of years, but they buried it deep enough that they didn't worry about big rains. Those coins wouldn't go anywhere, and next time they came this way – which would likely be in a few weeks – they would dig them up and split them between the two of them.

Norwood gave a chuckle.

"He probably skimped and saved his entire life for them old coins. Probably everything he had to get hisself started in the new territory. And like a danged fool, he pulled that bag out in front of strangers."

They'd seen the man with the sack of coins at his wagon. Collecting just a couple of coins to go into Bridger's trading post and buy some late supplies. Then he'd stashed the sack back in the wagon. What were they supposed to do? A man had to learn a lesson for his carelessness.

"It's money enough for him to make a fuss out of it," Rimmer said. "Maybe we was the careless ones."

"How so?" Norwood asked, chewing at his thumbnail.

"We got a big payday coming up with this wagon train," Rimmer said. "We could likely make ourselves a small fortune off these people. But we started trouble here that maybe we don't need."

A group of Indians encamped at the fort started a race. Five braves on horseback galloping out across the worn plain. A couple of miles out on the horizon, the Townes Party's cow column kept the livestock separated from all the others in the little bit of tall grass that remained near Bridger's. There were other pockets of livestock out on the horizon in different directions.

And now here came Elias Townes and his younger brother.

"Mr. Rimmer," Elias said, approaching. "We've determined that we should move out in the morning. Before sunup. Does that suit you?"

"Suits me fine. Me and my boys'll be ready." Rimmer tossed his head at the small mob of folks now entering Bridger's Fort. "There some trouble there?"

"They've accused one of our party of theft. A sack of coins has gone missing, and our man was apparently seen over near the wagon it went missing from," Elias said. "I know the man, having traveled all this way with him. He is no thief."

Rimmer made a grunt.

"You never can know a man. You can know the side of him he wants to show you, but you can't know his heart nor his mind. That's my experience."

"True," Elias said. "But I doubt very much this man is a thief."

17

"Is this trouble why you're all eager to move out come morning?" Rimmer asked.

"I'm not worried about this trouble. I'm just eager to move out. We've delayed here too long as it is," Elias said. "We have to worry about being caught by an early snow."

Rimmer nodded.

"You made a late start of it, indeed. But we'll get you where you're bound."

"Very good," Elias said. "Zeke and I will go and spread the word among the rest of our party. We'll find out now who intends to remain with us, though I'd wager it'll be the largest part of the group that came in with us."

"They ain't got much choice in the matter," Rimmer said. Elias had made Rimmer fully aware of the goings on since Fort Laramie that had disrupted his party of emigrants. He did not want Rimmer signing on with him without knowing. The banishment of his own brother, the enmity among some of the members of the party. What Elias did not know, and Rimmer knew well, was that such events were common among emigrant trains. Always some sort of bickering and in-fighting occurred. Rimmer had ridden along with several trains over the years. Quarrels and gripes, bitterness – it's what happened when you mixed together a variety of people like this.

As free and open as the terrain was from Missouri to Oregon, all these folks traveling in a wagon train were as caged as if they were in a prison. They did not dare wander away from the body of the wagon train. They might easily be lost for good. Chained together as such, they were bound to get a mite irritable with each other.

"I'll walk with you," Rimmer said, pushing himself off the log wall and leaving Norwood sitting there with the tip of his knife scraping grime out from under a fingernail.

When they were some distance from Norwood, Rimmer said, "Mr. Townes, I don't want to get off on the wrong foot with you. And so I feel compelled to make a confession to you."

Elias gave Rimmer a severe look. Nothing good would follow from that opening line.

"Truth of the matter is, my man Norwood over there – well, he's a rough sort, as you might expect to find out here in the wilderness. He ain't been with me long, and as I were saying about knowing a man, I can't speak to what's in his heart."

"Do you have doubts about bringing him with us?" Elias said.

"I do, indeed. Indeed. I do. Fact is, Mr. Townes, I seen that man leaving camp a while ago. Curious, I watched him. He walked about five hundred yards up yonder. I said to myself, now what's he doing? I seen him go to a cottonwood up on the horizon. Hell, I reckon you could see it from here. Yep. That one yonder. You see it there? He was up under that tree for a few minutes. Then he come back. I found that behavior to be a mite curious."

Elias took a heavy breath. The three of them, Elias and Rimmer, with Zeke on the other side of Rimmer, still strode out toward the wagon train, but Elias had slowed his gait some.

"What are you saying, Mr. Rimmer?"

"Well, now you come here talking about lost money – a sack of coins, you say? – and I can't help but wonder."

Elias stopped, straightening his back and looking up at the sky.

"You think Norwood stole the money?" Elias said.

Rimmer shook his head.

"Oh, no sir. No, sir. I wouldn't accuse. No, sir. But I find the series of events curious. You understand?"

Elias looked at his brother.

"Zeke?"

Ezekiel Townes pursed his lips and took a deep breath through his nose. He nodded his head. Then he peeled away from the other two and turned back, walking out toward the lone cottonwood on the horizon.

"LET ME BORROW THAT shovel," Zeke said to a boy outside the fort who was filling a wooden barrel with dirt and rock.

The boy looked to be about ten years old, dark skin and hair suggesting he was half Indian.

"I got to finish filling this barrel," the boy said.

The barrel was one of a dozen or more just like it sitting around the fort. They filled them with dirt and rock to the top, then built fires on the dirt and rock to provide light in the yard at night when the yard was full of wagon trains. Night watchmen would come along every so often a drop a log onto the fire. Not only did the fires in the wooden barrels light the yard, but they also helped to keep the summer bugs down and snakes from coming too near the fort. At least, that was Bridger's belief.

"I'll bring it back to you directly," Zeke said. "Go stand in the shade and have yourself a drink of water."

The boy gave an uncertain glance back at the fort and wrinkled his forehead at Zeke.

"Ol' Gabe wants this done," the boy said. "And I got another barrel yonder I got to fill."

Zeke pursed his lips and took a breath.

"Don't you want a drink of water, son? A couple of minutes in the shade?"

"Yeah."

"Then hand over the shovel and let me use it for a minute. Keep me from having to walk all the way back to my wagon."

"I don't know if I should," the boy said.

Zeke reached into his pocket and found a one dollar coin.

"Here, now you're richer for renting the shovel out, and you'll have a cool drink and a some shade. I'm just walking to that cottonwood yonder."

The boy looked out at the cottonwood.

"You don't need a shovel to walk to a tree."

"I need a shovel to walk to that tree," Zeke said. "Now turn it over afore I turn you over my knee."

The boy twisted his mouth and gave his head a small shake.

"Give me that coin," he said.

Zeke handed over the coin and the boy handed over the shovel. Zeke started out for the cottonwood.

Zeke noticed when he was about two hundred yards out from the fort that Norwood started to follow him. He paid the man no attention and continued on with his mission. He'd be looking for loose dirt, recently turned. If Norwood had buried something out here by the cottonwood tree, as Rimmer suggested, it would be easy enough to find.

Zeke had grown fond of the cottonwood trees. The leaves rattled like a thousand cicadas in the constant blowing winds out here on the wide plains. The rough bark, the soft wood, the rattling leaves had become welcome companions along the trail. They had them back home in Paducah, but they weren't nearly as common as the variety of oaks and hickory, beech and birch. And they were all but useless as timber wood at the sawmill. Too soft for construction. So Zeke had always ignored them back home. But out on the prairie, cottonwoods provided one of the few sources of shade. He'd sat beneath cottonwoods for many hours on this journey already, and figured he'd do so for many hours more as they continued on. More importantly, they also noted water on the horizon. How many times already had Zeke stood on a grassy hill, looked out over the horizon and seen the cottonwoods, looking more like bushes than trees, growing down in a little river cut – just the tops of them visible – and known they were approaching a water source for the animals.

This one in particular sat in a shallow ditch, a dry wash that probably only ran with water during the worst flooding seasons. Zeke walked directly along the little ditch, and even before he got to it, he saw a small mound of freshly turned dirt. A few sticks and a broken branch from the tree had been placed over the dirt to try to cover over it.

Zeke glanced back and saw Norwood quickening his pace, closing the distance between them.

He drove the shovel blade into the soft earth and it sank a couple of inches deep. He pushed it a bit deeper with his foot and turned it over. No question but that the ground had recently been disturbed. He raised the shovel up, hands over his head, and drove it down again. Pushed it further with his foot. Gave a look toward the fort and saw that Norwood was almost at a jog, now. Coming on fast. He'd seen what Zeke was doing, knew he was digging up the coins.

Zeke turned the dirt one more time, and this time when he scooped out the dirt, he could see a sack. He dropped the dirt on the round and grabbed the sack. It was lighter than he expected, but when he gave it a shake he could hear the coins rattle inside.

Norwood stopped, now probably just fifty yards away.

"This belong to you?" Zeke called to him.

"I ain't never seen that before," Norwood said.

"Uh-huh. Then how come you followed me out here?"

Now the man resumed his journey, at a walk, toward Zeke.

"What if I say that does belong to me?" Norwood asked, and now his hand was on the grip of a long-bladed fighting knife in a scabbard on his belt.

"Then I'd say you're a liar and a thief," Zeke said. As he said it, he looped the top of the sack into his belt and tied it off securely. The shovel leaned against his stomach.

"I'll show you your insides you say that about me again," Norwood growled. He'd come to within about ten feet of Zeke.

"You're a liar," Zeke said. "And a thief. And you won't be traveling with our party."

Norwood slid the knife from its scabbard. A wide, thick blade. A grip wrapped in a leather strap.

"You think I give one damn about traveling with your party?" Norwood snarled. "You hand over that sack, or I'll cut it out of your hand."

"I'll hand it over, but I intend to hand it to the man to whom it belongs," Zeke said. Zeke hefted the shovel up with one hand and took a step off to his side to show his intention to walk around Norwood.

"Where do you think you're going?"

"I'm going back to the wagon trains, going to find the man whose missing this sack, and I'm going to let them know at the fort that you're the man who took the sack."

"Like hell you are," Norwood said, and he hunched his shoulders, both hands wide in a fighting stance, ready to pounce on Zeke. He stood on the balls of his feet, shifting his weight from one leg to the other, shoulders moving to a slow rhythm.

"Put that knife back in its scabbard before you get yourself hurt," Zeke said.

Norwood was a wild looking man. Like Rimmer, he wore a light coat, probably of deerskin, that covered a shirt well-stained with nature. His boots and britches both showed plenty of wear. His wire beard stretched a fair way down his chest, and his long hair flowed below his shoulders. He had piercing blue eyes, now wide with anger.

"You'll be the one hurt," Norwood said.

The man lunged forward, thrusting the knife out in front of him, closing the short distance between him and Zeke.

Zeke had the shovel in both hands in an instant. He'd have preferred to get it high, over his shoulders, to get a bigger swing on it. As it was, he swung it up from the ground, and it clanged loudly as the blade of the shovel smashed into the knife.

Norwood let out a yelp and the knife flew from his hand.

"You broke my danged fingers!" he shouted, grasping the injured hand in his other hand.

Zeke didn't hesitate. He cocked the shovel back over his shoulder now and got the swing he'd wanted on it. The flat bottom of the shovel busted Norwood in the head.

The man went limp on his feet. His body just poured into a puddle on the ground. Instantly unconscious.

Zeke didn't know if he'd come to in a moment or an hour, so he stuck the shovel into the ground, grabbed Norwood by his ankles, and slid him over to the base of the tree. Zeke had knocked his hat clean off, so he picked that up and put it over Norwood's face. No need to let the man cook in Wyoming's July sun.

Zeke plucked the shovel from the ground and hiked back to the fort.

3

"MR. TOWNES, I SURE am sorry about that man," Neil Rimmer said. "I never was sure how trustworthy he was. When I heard about them missing coins and remembered seeing him out under that cottonwood tree, I suspected my suspicions was right."

Jim Bridger banished Norwood. Sent him off with a horse and a pack mule and told him never to show his face around the fort again. Norwood had supplies sufficient to get himself to Fort Laramie, and he made off to the east that afternoon. Thomas Hedden made some embarrassed apologies to Wiser McKinney who waved them off, though Wiser clearly harbored some bitterness over the issue.

"What's done is done," Elias Townes said. "Do you expect he'll come back, looking for revenge?"

"Oh, no. He ain't the sort," Rimmer assured. All the same, Elias sent word to the cow column and told them to be on the lookout through the night, and he and Zeke and some of the others took turns keeping watch, patrolling the wagon train's encampment.

Well before dawn, Elias began spreading the word through the wagon train.

"Get your teams hitched," he said, walking among the emigrants of his party. "We roll out in two hours."

Fires started to show up in the camp as the women cooked breakfast while the men trekked out to bring down the oxen. Sleepy children whined. Others wanted to go and play, but their mothers called them back to help with breakfast or at least keep them within sight.

A tension filled the air around the camp. Elias could feel it.

Every emigrant in the party understood that the long and tedious journey so far was nothing compared to what lay ahead. The last thousand miles would prove to be the most arduous. The hardest work was ahead of them.

"I'm glad to have you and your men with us," Elias told Rimmer that morning. Including Rimmer, there were seven of them – well, six now.

Already they were showing their worth. They pitched in without being asked. Hitching teams, driving oxen. Each man came with his own horse. They knew the work that had to be done. Rimmer assured Elias that he knew the trail ahead, having made trips to Oregon City in the past.

Beyond Rimmer and his men, the Townes Party had picked up three new wagons and the families attached to them. A man named Smith moving with his wife and two young sons and his elderly father occupied one of those wagons. They'd planned to go to California, but after talking with some of the people at Bridger's Fort, they'd changed their minds and decided on Oregon Territory, instead. The other two were neighbors from Illinois. Farmers, both of them, who'd intended all along to go to Oregon Territory but from Independence they'd found this wagon train bound for California and joined in with it, always expecting to find a new party once they got to Bridger's Fort. Walter Brown was one of the men – he had three teenage daughters and a wife. The other man, his neighbor, was Luke Suttle. Suttle traveled with his nephew Brian and Brian's wife, but had no children of his own.

Elias had expected to lose at least a couple of wagons from their party – at least Marcus Weiss – but instead they'd added three.

Henry Blair, the boy they'd hired back in St. Jo to help guide the wagon train, he was as honest as the sun and as eager to help as a man could be. Elias intended to offer him a job when they got to the end of the trail. But he'd never been west of Bridger's Fort, at least not far west of it. His use as a guide had expired. Rimmer's outfit would see them the rest of the way, and while Elias remained the elected captain of the group known as the Townes Party, he intended to lean heavily on Rimmer's expertise as a guide.

Three months of waking up in the morning and getting teams hitched and wagons rolling should have been sufficient to make this outfit efficient, but always some problem occurred, great or small. After almost a week at Bridger's, this morning they were greeted with more problems than their share.

Oxen wandered and refused to be led. When Henry Blair went to catch his horse, it stayed twenty yards out in front of him. He must have chased the thing for a mile before finally getting a rope on the horse. Henry! The man Elias had looked to as a guide. One of the best they had, despite his young age. And Henry couldn't get his horse to cooperate. Solomon McKinney, Wiser's brother, could not find his singletree and had every family near him looking for it. Finally, Wiser McKinney discovered he had two. Jeff Pilcher's wife, at the last minute, panicked that they'd not bought enough flour at Bridger's trading post. Poor ol' Jeff, he had to go into the fort and summon a man from his bed to help him with an order of flour and bacon.

Reverend Marsh woke with a pulled muscle. He believed he'd done it in his sleep and declared that it was Satan's attempt at preventing him from going to minister to the Natives. Rimmer and his crew got Marsh's wagon team hitched for him. Reverend Marsh had expressed misgivings to Elias about hiring on a new band of men with no one vouching for them. Marsh than confided to Elias that he was carrying a sizable sum of money – donations from several churches back home, not only for Marsh's ministry, but also donations for a physician who had established a mission at Walla Walla. But now, with Rimmer and his men getting the preacher's wagon hitched to a team, Reverend Marsh had forgotten his concerns.

With the sun sending a single beam of light over the eastern horizon, Elias Townes, mounted on Tuckee, called out, "Wagons, roll out!"

They'd only missed Elias's desired departure time by about an hour.

The wagons creaked and groaned, having been stationary for almost a week. The loads inside shifted and strained against the ropes tying them down. The animals breathed hard and grunted, wary at being hitched again. The children laughed and ran ahead, barking dogs chasing at their heels. Their mamas called to them, fearful of what they couldn't see in the dark of the early morning. The cow column already moving the livestock down to follow the wagon train, likely to get jammed up behind the train before all the wagons were moving. Chaos in a single file line.

Zeke rode up even with Elias, a wide grin on his face.

"What are you so danged happy about?" Elias said.

"This is it, brother," Zeke said. "The great adventure toward Oregon City. I've got chill bumps."

Zeke held out his arm, as if to prove it, but his shirt sleeve and the dark hid the chill bumps.

"We're bound now to the green valleys, yonder. We're on the precipice of a new start for you and me and for the Townes family. Generations from now, our lineage will be cutting timber in them Oregon valleys, and they'll say, 'We wouldn't be here now had it not been for Elias and Zeke.'"

"Huh," Elias grunted. "I hope generations from now they'll bless us for bringing the family this way and not curse us."

Zeke laughed.

"I have great expectations of what's to come, Elias. They'll say we blessed them. They'll say we made them wealthy and proud, built up a family in the west. They'll talk about how the family left Kentucky in the same we we talk about how our forebears left the Scottish borderlands and come to America. They'll say old Elias and Zeke brung us here."

Elias nodded his head and cast his eyes into the dark ahead.

"Indeed, brother. I hope you're right. For now, I'll just be satisfied to make more than ten miles today."

THEY SAT OUT NORTH from Bridger's Fort, through sagebrush and grass. Out past the lone cottonwood tree where Zeke had unearthed Hedden's money and sealed Norwood's fate.

Elias wanted to be on the trail before any of the other wagon trains encamped at Bridger's started out. The other parties bound for Oregon were of slightly larger size, and Elias believed the Townes Party could move faster than they and each day extend the distance between them. What he wanted was to come to river crossings before the other parties so as to avoid delays as much as possible. A river crossing, especially a large one, would be an all-day venture. But with another wagon train in front of them, a river crossing might become a two day venture.

Elias got his wish, but only just.

That party that Hedden was in, they were putting out their breakfast fires and hitching their teams just as the Townes Party began to roll out.

The trail here was simple to follow. A clearly worn path, ruts cutting into the hard-packed earth. A blind man could easily have followed this trail. If his toe kicked sagebrush, he'd know he'd put down a wrong foot and must simply adjust slightly.

Other than the sage, there wasn't much forage for the cattle. The grass through here had all been cropped pretty thoroughly by earlier wagon trains. As such, the animals didn't get much distracted and kept the wagons moving. It wasn't long before the rhythm of the trail began to feel natural again. For those walking along, one foot in front of the next. For those mounted, the lazy gait of the horse under them. The swinging chains and ropes on the wagons. The steady blow of the wind. The sun crawling up the sides of their faces. The sweat pouring from under hats.

The terrain began to look very much like that they'd crossed through the South Pass. Rolling hills of green grass and gray sagebrush, bright blue sky.

From atop his horse Duke, Zeke watched a storm gather to the northwest. The clouds seemed to melt to the earth, but Zeke knew that was buckets of water washing down over the landscape. That storm was probably two hundred miles away, probably covering an area of eighty or a hundred square miles, but it seemed like just a tiny thing in the hugeness of the vast, wide-open sky.

Elias saw the storm, too. He wondered if it was filling low spots along the trail somewhere, making the ground soft and preparing to mire them in. Elias tended to worry over such things, but Zeke didn't steer him away from those worries. The truth of it was, Elias planned for the worst of outcomes, but his philosophy left him prepared when calamity struck.

At a rise, distance enough from Bridger's that the fort could no longer be seen on their backtrail, Elias reined in and took a long look around.

"Would you look at this?" he said.

Zeke moved his eyes across the horizon. Everything blue sky and green grass, though a wide swath of grass was cropped near to the earth. Green as the countryside was through here, they'd have to walk the livestock two or three miles off the trail at the end of the day to find enough grass for the cattle and horses.

"What am I looking at?" Zeke asked.

"What do you see?"

Zeke chuckled.

"I believe I see land stretching out for a thousand miles."

"Maybe," Elias said. "But I guess the question I should ask is what don't you see."

Zeke thought about it for a moment. He wanted to get the question right, and so he tried to see the countryside through Elias's eyes. What were his concerns? Good grass. Water for the emigrants and the livestock. Rough terrain that would make for difficult passage.

There was grass enough. They'd walk to find it, but it was out there. They knew the water sources up ahead. Bridger had said there'd be creeks still with water in them, and soon enough they'd reach the Bear River Valley. Then they'd come to Beer Springs where some said the carbonated water tasted like beer. Bridger himself told Elias that the only people who thought the water tasted like beer were those who'd forgotten what beer tasted like.

And then they'd be along the Snake River, which they would follow for a considerable distance. Presently, water was not a concern.

"I don't see much in the way of rough ground, if that's what you're referring to."

"No," Elias said. "There ain't a tree. Not a single tree. Nothing taller than sage as far as you can see."

Zeke took another turn around the horizon in his saddle.

"Yep. You're right."

It wasn't their first time looking across the horizon and seeing no trees, but it seemed they'd done it so long now that it was starting to get to Elias.

"This ain't no place for a timber man," Elias said. "What are we going to do if we get to Oregon and there ain't no trees?"

"We've bought a timber lease," Zeke said. "The man we bought it from assured us there were more trees than we could cut in our lifetimes on that lease."

Elias nodded his head.

"He did make those assurances, and then he took our money and we will never see him again, even if we come back looking for him. I guess I'm just feeling a bit nervous now."

"Ah, don't worry about it, Elias. There'll be trees. And if there ain't, we'll be farmers."

4

THE TOWNES PARTY DID eighteen miles that first day out from Bridger's. Most of the day they could see another wagon train behind them, and Elias pushed them harder than maybe he should have, later in the day than he might typically. He wanted separation from that other wagon train. Already, proximity to them had caused trouble. Wiser McKinney nearly drowned for a theft he'd not committed.

The second day, they crossed a creek and that slowed them down a bit.

They only did about thirteen miles, and when they camped they could see behind them the campfires of the other wagon train, the one with Hedden in it.

The third day, the terrain grew rougher all around them. Hills rose on both sides. More up and down than they'd done the previous two days. Harder going, maybe, but nothing difficult. And again, Elias drove the wagon train farther and longer than he might ordinarily have done, hoping to continue to stretch the distance between the two trains.

The Townes Party managed to make somewhere close to fifteen miles on the third day out from Bridger's Fort, and Elias declared he thought it was just about the best three days in a row they'd had.

But Henry Blair on that third evening just at sunset rode down from the cow column to report some disturbing news.

"I think someone's trailing us," Henry told Elias and Zeke confidentially.

Zeke laughed.

"A whole train of wagons is following us, Henry."

The three of them stood near Elias's wagon where his wife Maddie was still cooking supper. Every family had collected firewood from around the creeks down near Bridger's Fort, and they had maybe two days left of firewood before they'd have to cook over buffalo dung.

"No, sir. I mean I think a single rider is trailing us."

"What makes you think so?" Elias asked.

"A couple of times today, I rode out away from the livestock to breathe some air. Both times, when I looked back, I could see something out on the horizon. The first time I was too sure. Maybe a couple of antelope or something. But the second time I was definite about it. I was seeing a horse and rider trailing another horse. Or maybe a mule."

Zeke frowned at Elias.

"Rimmer's man," Elias said. "What was his name?"

"Norwood," Zeke said.

"Bridger sent him east to Fort Laramie."

"Seems he's decided to go west," Elias said.

"Fort Hall is no farther to the west than Fort Laramie is to the east. Maybe he's staying close to us just in case he runs into Indians."

"Maybe," Elias said thoughtfully. "Unless Rimmer is giving him aid."

Zeke shrugged.

"It's possible. I haven't seen anyone go back at night."

"Nor have I," Elias said. "Where is Rimmer?"

Zeke looked around, but Henry Blair spoke up.

"He's back with the cow column. Made his camp with us."

"Norwood is free to go in any direction he wants," Zeke said reasonably. "Bridger sent him away from the fort, but he can't force him to make for the east."

"True enough," Elias said. "But I don't want him causing trouble for us. And Rimmer assured me he wouldn't."

Zeke grunted.

"Rimmer can't force him to stay away, neither. The man can go any direction he chooses."

"I don't know that I care much for him being on our backtrail," Elias said.

"I don't hardly see what trouble one man can cause us."

"Pass the word around with the people you can trust, Zeke," Elias said. "Make the men keeping watch tonight aware that Norwood might be out there."

"Sure," Zeke said. "But the man would be a fool to try to bother us."

"Henry, would you care to eat supper with us before you return to camp?"

"I'd be right pleased with that," Henry said.

Zeke left them to it.

Just about every evening, Elias and Madeline fed a small army there at their wagon. Elias's older daughter Margaret and her new husband Jason Winter were traveling with the wagon train. Jason had an injured leg and spent most of the day riding in the wagon. To help out, Madeline had combined Jason and Maggie's supplies with her own and was now feeding both families. In addition, she cooked for any number of the hired hands who drove wagons or helped with the cattle. And Elias and Madeline had four other children, Gabe and Chris, Martha and Mary. Every meal at Elias's wagon was like a Sunday supper with the cousins and neighbors.

But Madeline managed it like a trail cook. She avoided preparing too much supper which would lead to a waste of stores, but no one ever left their wagon hungry. Somehow, she seemed to accurately predict each night the numbers of strays who would turn up. This night, Henry Blair was the stray.

Zeke, meanwhile, made his way back to his wagon.

On purpose, every day as the wagons started out, Elias put his wagon at the front and Zeke's near the back. He liked having Zeke back there seeing to things. Zeke knew that Elias counted on him to watch for children and livestock wandering away while the wagon train was moving. He kept an eye for any problems – a broken wagon wheel or a faltering animal. He also tried to manage any disputes that arose among various families traveling with the party. Though having killed a man during a dispute and been banished, at least temporarily, from the wagon train, Zeke felt awkward about intervening in disputes.

The wagons now were circled, one tongue laying on the back of the wagon in front of it. The cow column had the oxen out now, grazing in the good grass, but soon they would lead them into the circle of wagons, keeping them like a paddock overnight. The other cattle and livestock they'd have to roundup in the morning, but the boys tending the livestock could do that while the wagons were getting started out. The oxen and the riding horses would need to stay inside the circle of wagons.

Zeke spoke to Solomon McKinney, Captain Walker, and Jefferson Pilcher, asking them to take turns on watch for the night and letting them know there might be a man following.

"Is it the thief who was banished from the fort?" Captain Walker asked.

"It could be," Zeke said. "That's my thinking, anyway."

Captain Walker was a veteran of the Seminole War, an Indian fighter from the east.

"We'd be wise to keep a watch on all those men your brother hired," Walker said. "If not for the necessity of an experienced guide, I would have recommended passing on those men."

Zeke came to Marcus Weiss and passed him by without a word.

Weiss had hired a new man to drive his team at Bridger's Fort. The man seemed competent enough, and not nearly as surly as Weiss or his former driver. He'd spoken to Zeke a number of times. Willie Cooper was his name. But that also freed up Caleb Driscoll to drive Zeke's wagon again. Caleb was just a few years younger than Zeke – Zeke still a young man himself and much younger than Elias, his oldest brother. Caleb was one of those who'd signed on with Elias and Zeke to work for them in the Pacific Northwest. Zeke paid him to drive his wagon, but from Fort Laramie to Bridger's Fort, Caleb had driven Marcus Weiss's wagon.

Now Caleb was back driving Zeke's wagon.

Marie spoke to Zeke in her slight accent. Her parents were French, though she'd grown up as Zeke's neighbor in Kentucky. Still, she spoke with an accent that wasn't easily discernible. Anyone familiar with American accents would know she wasn't Northern or Southern or Midwestern. They might guess she was French-Canadian, though there was too much Southern mixed with her French. Her soft voice, the foreign accent, her dark features, they all combined to make her very mysterious, and very much out of place on the Western Plains.

"Eat while your supper is still hot," she said. "Everything left is for you. We've all eaten."

"Thanks," Zeke said. "How are we on firewood?"

"No more wood on the fire tonight," Marie said. "If we're careful, maybe we have enough wood for three more fires."

Zeke sighed. If they passed near a creek, they probably could find some firewood tomorrow to add to what they had.

Zeke's family had brought a number of dogs along. Zeke liked having dogs nearby, especially with his young son Daniel a toddler and prone to wander. Dogs would warn of snakes near the camp. They'd follow the boy and make him easier to find if he got out of sight. Some of them were useful for herding the cattle. They were a warning of approaching danger – whether it be bad weather or Indians or bandits – and two or three among their pack would fight if the family was threatened.

And if worse came to worst, dogs would make for a food source before the oxen and the horses.

Among the dogs, Towser and Mustard were the best two. Towser, a black and white herder, and Mustard, a yellow dog with a stout build. They were smart dogs, instinctive. Both of them followed Daniel around wherever the boy went, and when Towser decided he'd strayed too far, the black and white dog would take Daniel by the cuff of his shirt and pull him back toward the wagon. Mustard didn't herd, but he'd start barking when he decided something was amiss.

Both dogs gathered with Zeke while he ate his supper. Stew made with potatoes, onions, carrots, and beef, the fresh beef bought from Bridger's Fort at a price high enough to have purchased an entire cow back east. Zeke plucked a couple of pieces of beef from his stew and gave one each to the two dogs.

"That's expensive meat to give to the dogs," Marie chided him.

"They're good dogs," Zeke said, and gave Mustard a scratch behind the ear.

With the wagons circled the way they were, Zeke's wagon was the farthest back. If a man tried to sneak up to the wagon train from behind, he'd likely encounter Zeke and his family first.

"Caleb?" Zeke said. "Tonight, you be sure of where that scattergun is."

Caleb cast a curious look at Zeke.

"You expecting trouble, Mr. Zeke?"

"Not expecting it, but I'd like to be ready if it shows up."

"I'll be ready."

"We'll take turns keeping watch tonight," Zeke said.

The wagon train party kept a watch every night. Usually just two or three men, awake and prepared to raise an alarm in case of trouble. Responsibility for night watch shifted among the various families of the wagon train, and tonight was not Zeke's night to keep watch.

"It ain't our night," Caleb pointed out.

"We'll stay up anyway," Zeke said. "And we're watching for folks to leave the wagon train as much as we're watching for folks to come into it."

The curiosity on Caleb's face grew, but he didn't ask any questions, and Zeke didn't say anything more.

"Mr. Zeke," Caleb whispered, pushing his hand into Zeke's shoulder.

Zeke opened his eyes to darkness. Everything black. He and Marie and Daniel bedded down on a thick bed of canvas and quilt they'd slid under the wagon. Zeke blinked, hoping his eyes might adjust to the darkness some and perhaps he could better see, but he could only make out the outline of Caleb Driscoll, blocking out the vast design of stars above.

"You wanted me to wake you," Caleb said.

Zeke grunted and rolled toward Caleb, out from under the wagon. He reached up and felt for the water barrel tied to the side and resting on a shelf fixed to the wagon. With his hand on it to guide him clear, he stiffly stood.

"Everything all right?" Zeke whispered.

"Yes, sir. It's been quiet all night. I've heard some coyotes, but nothing near us."

Zeke felt around until he found his saddle gun in a holster strapped to the back wagon wheel. He had to feel his way with his fingers to the buckle to release it, and he strapped the belt around his waist. His hat was shoved in between the spokes of the wheel, and he fetched that out, too.

"Go get some sleep, Caleb. I'll take the watch until morning."

The tedium of the trail was nothing compared to the tedium of a night watch on the trail.

Zeke wandered a short ways from the wagons, the vein of stars stretching across the night sky providing enough light to reveal shapes as black spaces on the horizon. A black hill here, a black horse there, a black wagon. Only the canvas covers glowed a sort of dirty brown.

But out across a wide stretch of ground, Zeke could see a pinprick of light cutting through the darkness. A lantern. Someone was walking out from the circled wagons toward where the cow column had made its camp. Whoever it was made no effort to conceal himself, the lantern bobbing and moving.

"Zeke Townes, is that you?" a whispered call came. Zeke recognized the voice as Captain Walker's, but he could not see the man.

"It's me," Zeke responded, turning toward the sound of the voice.

Walker moved several steps closer, and Zeke could see the movement. He was about thirty yards away, coming to Zeke from the direction of his wagon.

"Who is that walking out there?" Zeke said.

"Your brother," Captain Walker said. "I just spoke to him a few minutes ago."

"Everything all right?" Zeke said.

"He said he just wanted to check on the men out there to be sure they're all right."

Zeke guessed that the truth was Elias intended to try to catch Rimmer or one of the others going out to Norwood, to at least know if they had someone among them who couldn't be trusted.

"You haven't seen anyone else moving about?" Zeke asked.

"I've only been awake about an hour, but I've not seen anyone."

The two men stood together for several minutes, Zeke speaking of the rain he'd seen in the distance a day or two back and idly wondering if it would be sufficient to swell the Snake River when it came time to cross and Captain Walker commenting that he used to hate to see dark clouds in the sky when he was fighting the Indians in Florida. Captain Walker often had a way of bringing his conversations back to the Seminole Wars.

They were thus engaged when a shout broke the night's silence, followed by a woman's scream. And then the blast of a shotgun.

Zeke happened to be looking in the right direction and saw the discharge of orange sparks, and so he was able to run directly to the spot.

"What's the matter?" Captain Walker demanded when they were still twenty yards from where Zeke had seen the shotgun blast.

Someone was lighting a lantern. There were calls throughout the wagon train, people shouting to keep it down, others demanding to know what was going on. In a loud voice, some man from across the circle of wagons shouted, "Was that a gunshot?"

In a matter of seconds, the place had turned into a din of chaos, and Zeke had a thought lazily come to mind that out here in the great vastness of the prairie this little cluster of wagons had disturbed the natural peace of the land.

The disturbance came from camp where the Brown family slept. Walter Brown and his wife and three teenage daughters. Brown was a farmer from Illinois, neighbors there with the man called Suttle who traveled with his nephew and his nephew's new wife. The lot of them were bound for Oregon where they intended to again take up farming.

Now Brown stood with a scattergun in his hands. It was his wife who held a lantern, and the three daughters were huddled together, bathed in the light from the lantern.

"Mr. Brown?" Captain Walker said. "For what purpose have you fired that gun?"

"It was a rattlesnake," Brown said, and he pointed vaguely toward a patch of ground where all that set was his pair of boots.

At the claim of a snake, those nearby backed away. Brown's wife, who had a lantern lit now, also slid away, taking the light with her. Zeke took the lantern out of her hand and stepped nearer to the spot where Brown said there'd been a snake.

He stretched out, holding the lantern over the boots.

"I don't see nothing," Zeke said. He bent low, pushing the lantern toward the space beneath Brown's wagon. "Captain Walker, you want to shake out them blankets?"

"Not particularly," Captain Walker said. But he took his rifle barrel and started plucking the pallet of blankets from under the wagon, giving each one a shake in the lantern's light until he reached the canvas at the bottom. He lifted that, and Zeke flinched. But there was no rattlesnake among the blankets.

"It's awful cool tonight for snakes to be prowling," Zeke said. "Earlier in the night, when it's still warmer, that's when I'd expect to see them. Not now, though."

"Well, I heard something moving," Brown said.

Several folks were gathered round now from other wagons, and Zeke noticed Rimmer there among the crowd. He noticed him largely because he thought Rimmer was bedded down with the cow column.

"You ought not to shoot if you ain't laid eyes on what you're shooting at," Zeke said.

"Damned right," Captain Walker said.

"I swear I thought it was a snake," Brown said. "I heard something move and I reached for my gun."

"You killed the hell out of your boots," Zeke said with a slight chuckle.

He held up one of the boots, three big holes torn through the leather. A hole in the sole, too, showed that Brown was pointing the gun toward the ground from a slightly raised position – probably he slid from under the wagon and shot from his knees.

Brown took the boot from Zeke and examined it with a fair number of curses.

"It's my only pair of boots," he said. "How am I supposed to get to Oregon with a silver dollar sized hole in my boot?"

"Get used to having rocks in your shoes and blisters on your feet," Zeke said.

5

ZEKE SAT ATOP THE big gray horse he called Duke. He leaned forward, gave the animal a rub on the neck followed by a gentle pat.

"You just be strong today," Zeke cautioned the horse.

But his eyes were on the precipice, roaming the worn grooves in the hard-packed earth. Concern etched on this face.

They'd started the day camped on the south side of a creek right near its confluence with Bear River. Before sunup, wagons were rolling to ford the creek. They'd crossed a lot of shallow, narrow creeks over the last week, since leaving out of Bridger's Fort, but this was the biggest crossing they'd yet faced after leaving Bridger's. Time consuming, but not troublesome.

Neil Rimmer, though, did his first bit of guiding as the last of the wagons got north of the creek.

"In about five or six miles, it's going to get tougher today," Rimmer predicted, saying it to Elias but well within earshot of Zeke and a few of the others. "We'll have to cross the spur of a mountain. It'll be tedious getting up it, but it'll be treacherous getting down it."

And so it was.

They'd been following up through the Bear River Valley for about the last two days. Enjoying crystal clear, cool water from the many creeks. Enjoying lovely pastoral views of the big hills and mountains surrounding the valley. Not hardly enough timber in the whole valley to build a house, much less a settlement, but good land for farmers and such.

But around noontime, the wagon train arrived at the mountain spur. It reached down all the way to the Bear River. No way around. They had to go over.

And even with the worn traces of the wagons that had come before, they'd still had to pick their way up the hill. Cautiously twisting and turning the wagons through eroded washes, and more than once they had to put their shoulders into the sides of a wagon – six or eight men – to heave the thing up and over a boulder.

Tedious work. Slow going. Elias out front on his horse Tuckee choosing the way, directing those first few wagons. Zeke, Rimmer, Henry Blair, and some of the others riding up and down the wagon train to keep them all following the proper course and to lend a hand when necessary.

Slow going. Tedious work. The sun blazing down hot. But not terribly laborious.

Now, though.

Zeke shook his head in dismay. The wind blew hard up here on the top of the mountain spur, and every so often it would cut up under the brim of his hat and start to snatch it off his head. He'd have to reach up and slap a hand on it to hold it down, adjust it lower onto his head.

"Won't take much to lose a wagon coming down this hill," Zeke muttered, just loud enough for Elias to hear him.

Neil Rimmer was off his mount, walking at the top of the slope and looking over the edge.

The track was plain to see. Hundreds of wagons ahead of them had already cut the grass down to a ribbon of dirt.

"I could stand up here and look at this all day, but I ain't gonna find a better way down," Rimmer finally declared. "The way down the hills is the path right here – the way everybody's gone down before."

Elias nodded his head and took a heavy breath. He turned back to the wagons, many of them at a halt at the top of the hill but some still snaking their way up. Elias spoke in a loud voice for the benefit of those on the hill.

"You'll have to tie your wheels," he called out. "Rope or chain. Lock them so they won't roll. A wagon starts rolling down this hill, we won't catch it until we get to the Snake River. Nobody rides. Everyone has to walk. Every man will have to take turns walking a wagon down."

The work was exhausting. Elias appointed Zeke and Henry Blair and a couple of Rimmer's men with the task of checking all the wheels, making certain they were properly locked. Several times they had to retie knots or rework the ropes. They also made certain that the chains and ropes were secure on the first few wagons.

Elias had terrible imaginings of a wagon getting loose and plowing through a group of women and children below, so he decided that until they had at least a few wagons down the precipice, the women and children should stay back and wait to walk the descent.

At last, after a delay of probably half an hour or more, the first of the wagons started down over the side.

The work was troublesome. Zeke and Rimmer rode their horses, ropes on the back of the wagon and turned around their saddle horns. Six men – three to a side – held ropes and they lowered the wagon a step at a time. Every now and then, a man's footing would slip and he'd slide three or four feet down the steep hill. The oxen pulling the wagon had to be handled carefully. The man driving the team – in this case, it was Caleb Driscoll now driving Elias's wagon – had to keep his eye on every step the oxen took. The men on the ropes were almost fighting against the oxen, pulling the wagon back while the oxen pulled it forward.

Fifteen or twenty yards down the side of the slope, and Zeke was wondering if they'd spend the rest of the month trying to get the full wagon train down off of this mountain spur and moving along through the Bear River Valley again.

One foot at a time. The oxen bawling. Dogs running alongside the men, barking at this new and strange game the men were playing. The wagon straining to break free, to tumble ass over end and smash apart on the hillside. Men shouting or slipping, straining and sweating.

Elias atop Tuckee, watching the progress.

When his own wagon was maybe thirty yards down the hillside, Elias waved to the next wagon.

"Bring it on! Slow and easy! Just like this!"

And now two wagons on the face of the hill, a dozen men fighting against eight heavy oxen and all the pull that gravity could muster. Blistered and sweaty hands desperate to not let those ropes slide and burn loose.

Jason Winter, Elias's son-in-law with a wounded leg, had to be helped atop a horse, and he painfully rode the slope.

Elias quickly decided on about four teams of men to do the hard work. Mostly, he picked the crew who came with him and Zeke – Caleb and the Tucker brothers, Jerry Bennett and William and Cody Page – and Rimmer's men. It meant for these unlucky ones several trips up and down the hillside.

When they had about nine wagons down, Elias allotted to some of the other men the chore of helping down the women and elderly among their group.

With the women and children coming down in shifts behind the wagons, after a time, they had a fairly sizable crowd down below as well as a number of wagons and people still up above.

This is where they were when Noah Bloom lost his footing while walking his wagon down the slope.

"I DON'T WANT YOU to handle the wagon," Sophie said.

Sophie Bloom had no illusions about the man she married. He was a kind and loving man. Gifted as a speaker, strong in his own way. But he wasn't like the Townes brothers or the men who worked for them. He wasn't like the new guide and his men – rough men with rough hands and sun beaten faces. Even young Henry Blair or Caleb Driscoll, these were men who rode horses and pushed cattle and intimidated the great, hulking oxen with just their voices.

Noah Bloom was a good man, a good father, a good husband. But he was not one of these men.

"I've got to do my part," Noah chided her. "I can't let these other men do all the things while all I do is help an old woman and a pregnant woman walk down a hill."

"The old woman is your mother-in-law and the pregnant woman is your wife, and without your help neither of them could make this journey."

He'd helped the women, in his kind way, the way he'd done it since they first crossed the Missouri.

Betty Carlisle was Sophie's mother, and Abigail McKinney's. It was the McKinney brothers, Solomon and Wiser, who made the decision to take their families west to Oregon City. Let them go, Sophie thought. She would miss her sister, but let them go. Betty Carlisle, who lived with Sophie and Noah, she started mourning the loss of her eldest daughter the moment Abigail announced her husband's intention to go west. All of them understood it would be a forever parting. People who made that arduous trip west did not return to have to make it again. And Betty Carlisle was not interested in a forever parting from her first daughter.

It was Sophie's mother whispering at Noah about the opportunities in the west that finally convinced Sophie's husband that maybe Oregon Territory called also to him. Wiser and Solomon welcomed the notion.

Sophie never was so sure.

Wiser and Solomon were older. Noah thought a lot of them, looked up to them, and he convinced himself that if they were for it then it must be right.

With the day of departure nearing, Sophie Bloom's misgivings grew. And when it fell that she was pregnant, she thought surely her husband would abandon the idea. She even suggested waiting a couple of years. But Noah insisted. Pregnant women made the journey. So many people have gone already, he told her, the trail is downright civilized. Tamed. That had been the word he'd used.

How many times already had she seen her husband grab a rifle?

When Indians rustled the livestock. When bad men appeared on the trail ahead. Noah had been first among the emigrants to join with Elias Townes, ready to fight. Even when Wiser and Solomon stood back with the women, Noah rushed ahead with the rough men.

He needn't become involved in lowering the wagons, but he insisted that he would help. After seeing to Mrs. Carlisle and his wife, Noah trudged up the steep incline, back to the top of the mountain spur. Stubbornly he went.

And now, Sophie watched from down below. Her stomach plenty round. Their three young children playing nearby with some of the other children. She watched holding her breath.

"Easy there!" Caleb Driscoll called to the oxen, his voice even and unhurried. Calming the beasts.

The wagon wheels had swung wide, up out of the deep ruts cut into the ground. The men on the low side dug in their heels and tried to get it back. Noah had no tension in the rope he was holding at the front of the high side. The wagon was even a little behind him as he perched on a hill. The rope slack.

"Help us lower it!" one of Rimmer's men shouted angrily at him. He'd seen how often Noah held a slack rope, and it was agitating him. He'd two or three times called an angry order at Noah.

Noah reached low to pull the rope taut.

The wagon wheels skidded through the loose sand, dropping violently back down into the worn ruts. Noah lost his footing at the same time, over compensated and then pitched forward as the whole wagon jerked.

The commotion spooked the animals and the oxen bounded forward and the wagon smashed hard against Noah's head knocking him to the ground.

"Hold it!" Zeke shouted.

But too late.

The wagon wheel skidded right over Noah Bloom's limp body, crushing his chest.

Even from high up on the hill, the men working could hear Sophie Bloom's scream.

THEY BURIED NOAH BLOOM at the base of the hill where he'd lost his life. His was not the only grave they saw there.

Reverend Marsh spoke some words over him while Elias and Zeke and Henry Blair piled rocks over the body. The oldest of the Bloom children wasn't but six years old, hardly old enough to know what was happening. Sophie Bloom had not recovered from the shock of seeing her husband killed and did not attend the makeshift funeral. Instead, she sat in a camp chair in the shade of a wagon and alternated between weeping and staring in dismay out across the Bear River.

"What will we do about her wagon?" Solomon McKinney asked Elias when the funeral was finished and Noah Bloom was buried.

Elias grunted an answer that was no answer.

"She's your sister-in-law?" Elias asked.

"That's right. My wife Abigail is her older sister. But I can't hardly be responsible for her wagon and mine."

"No. I wouldn't expect you to be," Elias said. "How old a woman is she? About twenty-eight?"

"She's twenty-four years old."

Elias nodded.

"What prospects does she have when she reaches Oregon City?"

Solomon shook his head sadly.

"You know as well as I do," he said. "I'll do what I can for her, obviously. She's my wife's sister, so I'll be obliged to help her along. But three children, another on the way. I'll have my hands full enough with my own family – and I'm sure now my mother-in-law."

Elias nodded his head.

"Plenty of unattached men in Oregon Territory," Elias said. "Best hope she'll have is finding one who don't mind taking on another man's children."

Solomon scoffed.

"They shouldn't have tried this journey," he said. "Not with her pregnant. And Noah? Well, Noah maybe wasn't a man cut out for this. From today's vantage, I realize now that I should have discouraged him coming along."

Elias winced. He'd liked Noah Bloom pretty well. What Noah lacked in physical strength he more than made up for in moral fortitude. He'd shown himself, at least to Elias, to be a man of inner determination. When a band of Shoshone ran off the livestock, Noah was out in front with rifle in hand to go and fetch them back. He'd never been slow to throw his back into whatever job presented itself on the trail.

"I think he was cut out all right," Elias said. "We've passed graves enough to prove that accidents can happen to anyone."

Solomon nodded his head.

"Perhaps so. But we're still left with the trouble of what to do with Mrs. Bloom's wagon. I could take on some of her supplies and we could leave the wagon."

Elias waved away that idea.

"No. That won't be necessary at all, Solomon. I'll have Cody Page see to her wagon for the remainder of the journey."

Cody was about twenty-seven or twenty-eight years old, unmarried, and a good sort. Sophie Bloom was a pretty enough woman. Elias didn't care much if an attachment formed between them, but he figured he'd put Cody on her wagon and at least create the opportunity.

"But I'll only require Cody to help her get her wagon to Oregon City," Elias quickly added. "Whatever other needs she might have – including the children and her mother – those are things that family should see to."

Solomon nodded.

"I reckon that's me. I'm the family."

Elias gave him a grin and a pat on the shoulder.

"Indeed, Mr. McKinney. You're the family."

Elias waved Zeke over. They'd been another three hours bringing down the rest of the wagons and dealing with the burial. Daylight was running away from them, and the cow column was just now bringing the livestock down the hillside.

"I don't want to camp at a grave of one of our own," Elias said to Zeke.

"I can agree with that," Zeke said, giving a glance over his shoulder. Sophie Bloom now sat on her knees over at the rocks the Townes brothers had covered over her husband's body. A hand gently rested on one of the big, smooth stones that had come from near the river. "Will she come if we keep moving?"

"She'll have little choice," Elias said. "If we can get two more miles today, I'd be satisfied with that."

Zeke nodded.

"Go and fetch Cody. I'm going to ask him to drive Mrs. Bloom's wagon.

Zeke nodded and then gave his brother a sideways glance.

"Cody? He's a good man."

"Right. He can handle an ox team, and he's a good man. That's why I had him in mind."

"I don't mean he's a good hand," Zeke said. "I mean a good man. A decent man. The sort that would take on the responsibility of a widow and her children."

Elias grinned.

"Yes, Zeke. That's why I had him in mind."

"Might be a little soon for courting," Zeke said, casting another glance at Sophie Bloom.

"If we were on the east side of the Missouri River, I'd be inclined to agree with you. But I think we're going to find out that on this side of the Missouri, you can't waste much time on life's troubles. They'll come fast enough on their own. Anything you can do to improve your lot out here, you probably should be quick about it. But one way or another – if it's too soon or if it ain't – none of that makes a difference to me. I'm just trying to see to it that the woman and her children and that wagon make it where I said they would make it. I'm responsible for these people's lives, and I lost one today. I ain't looking to play matchmaker. I'm looking to not lose another life that I'm in charge of."

"I'll go and tell Cody," Zeke said. "You can give Mrs. Bloom your speech about hurrying to anything that will improve her lot in life."

Elias took a breath as Zeke walked away and watched for several moments the woman kneeling at the grave of her husband before finally feeling he could walk up to her.

"I'm sorry about your husband, ma'am," Elias said.

"I told him not to try to help with the wagon," Sophie said without looking up.

"That's the sort he was, though. Eager to pitch in. It's a good quality in a man."

"I suppose. I had a feeling, though. I wish he'd have listened to me. I just had a feeling he should leave it to others. When he rode off with you after those Indians that stole our cattle, I didn't have any qualms about that. Or when we encountered those men at the South Pass and he got his rifle and joined you. But today, I just did not think he should be helping with the wagons."

Elias nodded his head, though Sophie Bloom had still not looked at him.

Elias didn't have any words for this. Now that he was here, he'd have preferred to have given Solomon McKinney this job.

"It's a pleasant place where we buried him," Elias said. "The river and the mountains yonder."

"It's a pretty spot, I suppose. If a man has to be buried. But one place doesn't matter much from another. He'll never take in the view."

"No, ma'am. But maybe when you think on it, you'll remember."

Sophie nodded her head.

"I'll remember," she said.

"We need to move on, though. We need to get another couple of miles out of the day."

Sophie shut her eyes and nodded her head. She still seemed in a daze.

"I've arranged for Cody Page to drive your wagon," Elias said.

"I knew you would see to it, Mr. Townes. You're very kind."

Elias shrugged.

"Will you help me up?"

Elias held out a hand and felt her tiny fingers. She had no weight as she pulled herself up. She brushed off the knees of her dress and then frowned at Elias. She straightened up with a small groan and then put both hands on her belly.

"What will I tell his child?" she asked.

"You can tell the child that his father was a good and decent man and that he did his best," Elias said.

"You think it will be a boy?"

"Oh, I couldn't judge," Elias said. "I was just speaking hypothetically."

Sophie nodded her head.

"It might be a boy," she said. "I wonder what I and my children will do when we arrive in Oregon City without a husband and a father. What hope do we have?"

"You don't worry about that just now," Elias said. "Let's worry now about getting you there safe and sound, and the children. Once we're there, I'll make sure you're taken care of. You and the children."

She gave her head a small shake.

"We're not your burden, Mr. Townes."

"No, ma'am. Not a burden. But I won't let no harm come to you. For now, you rely on my man Cody. Mr. Page is a good man, and he'll get your wagon on to the territory without a problem."

Elias cinched the saddle on the palomino and stepped into the stirrup.

"I need to go and get the wagon train moving," he said. "You'll be along presently?"

"I will."

It took another half hour, but the wagons started to roll. Sophie Bloom stayed where she was for some time, but as Zeke's wagon passed by her, she at last turned away from her husband's grave and started walking to catch up to her children, now being corralled by the McKinney families.

6

"I CAN'T WALK ANOTHER step. Look at my foot."

Walter Brown held his foot up where Elias could see it in the light from the lamp.

"Yes, sir. That's painful looking," Elias said.

Brown had shot his boot all to hell three nights back, and now he had terrible blisters where the sole of his foot rubbed against the holes in his shoe.

The rays of the early morning sun showed beyond the mountain spur, marking the place where the afternoon before they'd buried a man. Elias found it difficult to muster much in the way of sympathy over a man's blistered feet when he considered the prospects in front of young Sophie Bloom.

"Maybe you should ride in the wagon for the day," Elias suggested. "Maybe spend the day patching that shoe."

"Patch it with what?" Brown demanded.

"Mr. Brown, I ain't the one who shot your boots all to hell," Elias said. "Don't get angry with me."

Brown took a heavy sigh. The man was making the journey with no saddle horse, as many others had done. If he could ride a horse, that would get him as far as Fort Hall. But without a horse, he almost had to walk. Nobody rode long in a wagon if they could help it. Some among them were equipped with a driver's box, though in many of them, a man would just have to find a place to sit among his belongings. But the wagons were bouncy, jarring things, even over the best of ground.

"I ain't mad at you, Mr. Townes. I just don't know what I would use to patch a shoe with a hole in it."

Elias looked around at the wagons, the men getting their teams hitched.

"Go and talk to Captain Walker. Have you met Captain Walker?"

"I have."

"He's got some strips of tough leather. You might be able to cut a piece to fit inside your boot. You could nail that into the sole and tap down the nails. I ain't saying it would make for the most comfortable shoe, but you might find it better than what you've got."

"Well, let me ask you a question, Mr. Townes. I didn't think of it until last night, and I should have considered it when it was a more readily available solution. But the man who died yesterday? Was his feet particularly large?"

Elias groaned and narrowed his eyes. He knew what Brown was suggesting.

"Why do you ask?" Elias said.

"Well, I was thinking I might borrow your horse and ride back and get the man's shoes."

Elias drew a breath.

"Mr. Brown," he said. "I find that extremely distasteful."

"Did you remove his pocket watch and give it to his wife before you buried him?" Brown asked.

"I did."

"How is this any different? The shoes ain't doing him no good now."

Elias couldn't quite find the words to say to the man why he thought the proposal was distasteful. He just knew that he didn't like it. Seeing Elias pause in his argument, Brown kept on.

"I could ride back, get them shoes, and catch back up before the wagon train has had time to make it more than a mile," Brown said. "I'll pay the widow for the shoes, if that puts your mind at ease."

Elias shook his head, but his resolve on the matter was broken.

"You'd be disturbing the grave, Mr. Brown. I don't care for that. But if you offer to buy the shoes from Mrs. Bloom, and if she accepts the proposal, I'll lend you one of my saddle horses to ride back."

"Fair enough," Brown said.

"But you'll cover the grave back over in a manner sufficient to keep animals out of it."

They'd been able to dig only a shallow grave in the hard-packed soil, but they'd been diligent about piling large stones over it.

"I'll go and talk to the widow," Brown said.

Elias watched Brown limp away.

It seemed a ridiculous thing to him that out here on this trail with hardly no folks around for miles and nothing but land and sky, mountains and rivers, a wagon train boss could be so harassed. But so it was. A thousand little particulars could disrupt his day, and would. Even a tiny band of emigrants – just around a hundred people when wives and children were counted – and yet still they could produce ten times their number of troubles during the course of a day. Some more troublesome than others.

Even as Walter Brown limped his way toward Sophie Bloom, Elias saw Henry Blair riding toward him. Elias took a few breaths as he watched the young man.

"Morning, Henry."

"Morning, Mr. Townes."

Henry didn't bother to drop down from his saddle. He'd be riding back to the cattle momentarily. They'd kept the cattle close to the wagons the previous night, this country being overrun with Shoshone, plenty of whom were hostile toward the settlers cutting through their territory.

"I saw a light again last night. I figured it to be about two miles distant."

"About at the mountain spur?"

"Yes, sir. That's where I figured it to be. I reckon it was a campfire."

Elias nodded.

That night he'd gone out to the cow column – the same night Walter Brown shot up his own boots thinking they were a rattler – Elias had seen nothing on their backtrail. Neither did he see any evidence of anyone leaving the cow column to provide assistance to the man following. So far, Elias only had reports from Henry and some of the others that there was someone back behind them.

"Keep watching," Elias said. "You haven't seen anyone go to help the man?"

"No, sir. And I've told some of the others to keep an eye open. Jerry and Will Page. But neither of them have seen anything to suggest Rimmer's men are riding back to take him food or anything. Of course, they gave the man plenty of supplies when they sent him off from Bridger's Fort. He could make it to Fort Hall on his own without any assistance from anyone in our wagon train."

"All right. Well, keep watching for me, Henry."

Henry nodded his head, dragged reins and started off back toward the cow column.

Elias took up Tuckee's reins and walked a ways along the circled wagons.

Captain Walker had his team hitched.

Marcus Weiss and his new driver were still getting their team together. Mrs. Weiss kept the children with her, out of the way. Elias couldn't help but curl his lip in disgust at the sight of the Weiss children. What kind of man forbids his children from playing with the other children around?

Jeff Pilcher and his wife were working their oxen into the yokes. Jeff's oldest son was helping, while the two younger children chased a couple of Zeke's dogs around.

"Don't wait for me!" a voice called out to Elias. "I'll catch back up."

Elias turned and peered over Tuckee's back. He saw Walter Brown, mounted on Noah Bloom's horse.

"The widow approved the deal," Brown said, leaning forward in Noah Bloom's saddle and shouting to Elias in a mock whisper. "I'll be back presently, and properly shod."

Elias gave a small wave.

"I'm pleased for you, Mr. Brown," Elias said.

Zeke and Caleb Driscoll had the team in place and ready to move. Zeke's horse was saddled.

"Morning, Elias."

"Morning, Ezekiel. I wonder if you might do me a favor?"

"I might, if it ain't a nuisance to me."

Elias chuckled.

"It'll be a nuisance, I can promise that. Walter Brown is riding back to Noah Bloom's grave, planning to get his shoes."

"Like hell," Zeke said.

"He bought them from Sophie Brown," Elias said. "At least, I hope he did. But he's getting them with her approval, at any rate."

"I assume the favor is to shoot him for grave robbing?" Zeke said.

"No. The favor is to ride back there and make sure he doesn't get into any trouble with whoever that is following us."

Zeke took a heavy breath.

"Elias –" he started, but Elias held up a hand to stop him.

"It don't sit right with me, neither," Elias said. "But if he's paying Sophie Brown for the shoes, it ain't up to you or me to get in the way of her doing what she can. If selling her dead husband's shoes helps her, then she should sell them."

"All right," Zeke agreed.

"Also, since you're going anyway."

"Uh-huh?"

"Make sure that man does an adequate job of piling the rocks back on top of that body."

"IF WE MAKE GOOD distance today and tomorrow, we'll camp tomorrow night at the beer spring," Rimmer said, riding near to the palomino.

Elias nodded his head.

"I'd like to do nothing less than twenty miles today," Elias said.

"It's easy going through this valley now, after getting past the spur. You'll want to plan to camp a day or two at the springs. There's hot springs, plenty of shade trees. It's a pretty little spot. You can bake the lightest bread you've ever tasted from the water straight from the springs. Those hot springs are a good spot for laundry, too."

Elias considered it for a moment.

"I'm eager to reach the end of our journey, Mr. Rimmer. But I suppose if we push hard for the next two days, everyone will be ready for a rest for a day or two."

Rimmer gave his horse a tap with his reins and the horse trotted out ahead of the first wagons. Elias watched him go, keeping Tuckee at a walk.

Madeline rode her pony this morning, though she often liked to walk in the mornings before the heat of the day.

Their two daughters, Martha and Mary, were back helping to look after some of the younger children in the wagon train. They'd both been good about caring for the younger children and doing so without being asked. Martha had said to Elias that looking after children helped to while away the time.

"Mr. Rimmer says the water from the springs up yonder is good for baking bread," Elias told Madeline as he rode up near her.

"Is it?"

"That's what he says. Lightest bread you've ever tasted."

"Will we rest long enough to find out?" Madeline asked.

"We will. Spend a day or two at the springs, is Mr. Rimmer's thinking."

"And you're not opposed to that?"

Elias sighed heavily and shook his head.

"I don't think I'm opposed to it."

He cast a look back over his shoulder. He could not see the farthest wagon back, though the cow column had reached a tall rise, and he could see the men pushing the livestock. Here and there, children laughed and played. Mamas called them back nearer the wagon train. The faces he could see, most of them, looked bright and full of hope. Untarnished from the loss of one of their own the previous day. But his eyes fell on Cody Page, walking alongside the ox team belonging to Sophie Bloom. Elias did not have to seek to find Sophie among the other people walking. She was there near to Cody, her young face etched with worry. Her belly stretching against her dress. The white bonnet covering her head like a halo in a painting, the morning sun catching it and making it glow.

His own daughter, Mary, walked with the Bloom children. They were too young to fully grasp what it would mean for them to lose their father. Hardship, probably. Unless their mother found a man who would take them in, give them a home. A woman alone in a rough and untamed territory had few prospects.

"I can't help but think of you when I look at Sophie Bloom," Elias said. "If something happened to me."

His thought trailed off.

"Don't seek trouble," Madeline chided him. "And you know that your brother wouldn't let anything happen to me and the children. And Jason is with us, as well. I would be well cared for."

"I don't know that Solomon McKinney sees Mrs. Bloom's troubles as his responsibility the way Zeke would take responsibility for you."

"Perhaps not," Madeline said. "His wife's sister? He must already be thinking that he'll have to take in his mother-in-law."

"He said as much to me yesterday."

"And Mrs. Bloom – pregnant – and with all her children? It must seem like a tremendous burden to him."

"Yes. I think so."

"Well, it was kind of you to put Cody Page on her wagon. Don't think I don't notice what you're doing."

"Cody could stand to have a woman settle him down," Elias said.

"That he could. Both those Page boys are a little wild for my tastes."

"We've a thousand miles to go yet," Elias said. "A lot can happen in a thousand miles."

"Perhaps I'll suggest to Mrs. Bloom that she should bake Cody some bread to thank him for helping with her wagon," Madeline said.

Elias grinned at her.

"Are you playing matchmaker now?" he asked.

Madeline returned the sly grin.

"No more than you are, Mr. Townes."

The boys, Gabriel and Christian, kept Elias's wagon moving at a good pace. His instruction to them was to be sure to set a pace that would not force any wagon behind them to have to slow down. Over the course of the day – barring obstacles that caused the wagons to bunch up – Elias wanted his wagons to widen the gap between the other wagons over the course of the day.

Depending what was counted, Elias had responsibility for the first four wagons in the train. His own, which ran out front. Usually his sons drove that wagon. It carried the family's supplies for the trail and furniture for making a home when they settled. Not much in the way of possessions. Johnny Tucker drove the second wagon. This was saws and blades and tools for the business. Elias considered this one more important by far than anything in the first wagon.

Jason Winters followed in the third wagon. Elias's son-in-law, injured in the leg during a scuffle with bandits. Christian had helped Jason handle the wagon some, but Jason was riding in the wagon and driving the team. He handled them just fine. Then it was Johnny Tucker's brother, Billy, who drove the wagon that carried all the possessions for both Johnny and Billy. Both of them were married – Anna and Josie, respectively, but neither of the Tucker boys had children yet.

After Elias's two wagons and the two belonging to people directly con-nected to him, the others started. The McKinneys – Solomon and Wiser – with their families. Then Sophie Bloom's wagon. Reverend Marsh fol-lowed behind Sophie Bloom. Then came the three new families. Walter Brown with his wife and teenage daughters, every one of them a pretty girl and soon they'd be coming into marrying age. The oldest might be there already. Jeb Smith traveling with his wife, two sons, and his elderly father. Luke Suttle in a wagon with his nephew and his nephew's wife.

Next in the line was a family called Grant who kept mostly to themselves. A man and wife, four sons and two daughters in the middle of the sons. The two older boys were in their late teens and pitched in with every chore. The daughters looked after the two younger boys. They were going to farm in the territory, and Elias figured they'd make a good go at it with so many farm hands. Grant had a fair number of good dairy cows in the cow column, and he was desperate to keep as many of them alive as possible for the length of the journey.

Then the Gordons. Mr. Gordon was probably around thirty years old. They had a couple of younger children, probably around eight years old. A boy and a girl. Mrs. Gordon was kept busy with a one-year-old daughter. When she was keeping the child, she kept busy spreading gossip among the column of wagons.

A family named Norton followed the Gordons, and then a family called Barnes.

There were another almost score of wagons beyond the Barnes family. Elias knew them all by name and remembered them by whatever problem they'd brought to him. And they'd all brought their share. A broken strap or a broken wheel.

A man named Long was there among the packers. Alone, probably about twenty-five years old. Bound to find work out west. Elias had already decided that if Long was interested, he'd hire him to work for the timber company when they arrived in Oregon. He was a solid worker who didn't complain overmuch. Long rode a black horse and led a mule packed with his gear. He was one of a half-dozen of packers who'd joined the wagon train back in Missouri. All of the packers were single men, and Elias figured they were all probably fleeing warrants back east. But they pitched in and helped when the going got tough, and in the evenings they all tended to find a family to eat with. Long was especially good at it. Elias didn't think that man had once broken into his own supplies to feed himself.

The packers tended to bunch up as a group together, though sometimes they'd be spread out among the wagons.

Captain Walker usually fell in behind the packers, and then came Jeff Pilcher. Jeff Pilcher was also a farmer and brought two wagons, one with personal possessions and the other with the tools of his trade.

Marcus Weiss and his wife – the people who had caused Elias the most trouble on this journey.

Then Zeke's wagon at the rear of the wagon train. Elias's youngest brother. A decade separated them in age. Elias with a daughter married, closer in age to Zeke and Marie than Zeke was to Elias. But they'd worked well together. Of all his siblings, Elias was glad that Zeke was the one out here with him, making this trip and preparing to build a business in the new territory.

Elias had stopped on a small rise, watching the wagon train as it passed him by. He smiled and nodded, waved to the emigrants as they passed. But he was lost in his own thoughts. Thinking about these families. More than thirty wagons representing something close to sixty families when the packers and drovers and now Rimmer's men were counted. More than a hundred souls, all looking to Elias to take them through a thousand miles of the roughest country on the continent.

Some had been with them from Missouri. A couple of them they'd picked up at Fort Laramie. Rimmer and his men, and three families joined them at Fort Bridger.

They'd had some go-backers in Kansas, where they'd also lost a child who wandered off. And now Noah Bloom was dead.

But Elias felt he'd done well to get so many so far.

As they passed him by, he wondered if he'd lose more.

And now he saw Zeke and Walter Brown returning, riding out wide past the livestock that followed the wagon train. He could breathe a little easier knowing his brother was back with them and no strays were spread out in the valley.

Dogs barked. Wagons rolled and creaked. Chains thunked against boards. Oxen groaned. Children laughed.

It was like a rolling city, Elias thought. A tiny civilization rolling across a ceaseless land, unfolding itself with every mile, under a ceaseless blue sky.

"Did Mr. Brown obtain his shoes?" Elias asked as Zeke's gray horse stepped up near him.

"He did," Zeke said with a wry grin. "Complained that the boots were mite tight on his feet. Cramped his toes. But he swore they were better than shoes with holes and that he'd stretch them out."

"Well, I'm pleased for Mr. Brown. Any sign that someone camped there overnight?"

"No question that someone is following us," Zeke said, lowering his voice as a family walked past alongside their wagon. "I saw a campfire about a hundred yards from where we buried Noah Bloom. Still warm this morning."

Elias nodded his head.

"But you didn't see the man?"

"No. I figure he saw me and Brown riding toward him from a distance and rode down behind a hill somewhere to hide from us. But there were fresh tracks there around the campfire. Looks like a single man with a horse and a mule."

"Norwood," Elias said.

"I would think so."

"You don't think he's looking for revenge after you found him out as a thief?"

"If he is," Zeke said darkly, "he'll have a tough time extracting it."

Elias nodded and then noticed that Neil Rimmer was riding over to them. Elias wondered at that. Did he know that Norwood was following them? Could he guess that Zeke had found evidence? Was he coming over to find out what Zeke had to report? Rimmer reined in as he came up even with Elias and Zeke.

"Mr. Rimmer," Zeke said in greeting. "I was just telling my brother that I saw signs of someone following us."

"Did you?" Rimmer said.

"My guess is that it's your friend Norwood," Zeke said. Zeke – right up front about it. No beating around the bush with him. Elias would have come at it with more tact.

"Could be Norwood, but he's no friend of mine. We was partnered up for a while, same with the others in my outfit. But you partner up with an outfit out here if you don't want to get scalped by Injuns. It ain't got nothing to do with friends."

"My concern is that he might intend to harass us in some way," Elias said.

"I wouldn't worry none about that," Rimmer said dismissively. "He's probably just going on to Fort Hall. It never was his intention to go back east, and when Bridger told him to make for Fort Laramie, I wondered about that. Going on to Fort Hall, staying close to us because he probably figures the Indians will leave him alone if he's near to a body of people."

"Uh-huh," Zeke said. "You don't think he means to harass us?"

Rimmer shrugged his shoulders.

"I couldn't say, but he's just one man. And I don't know what profit he would find in it."

"He could be holding a grudge against me. I did wallop him with a shovel."

"Well, that you did," Rimmer agreed with a chuckle. "But even so, one man ain't likely to attack an entire wagon train. If it bothers you, him being back there, me and a couple of my men could ride back and fix him."

"Fix him?" Elias said.

"Cut his throat. Bury him."

"Good Lord, no," Elias said. "We don't need to cut a man's throat."

Rimmer shrugged.

"If it eases your mind, we can take care of him."

"Thank you, Mr. Rimmer," Elias said. "I don't think that will be necessary."

"Just to be clear," Zeke said, going in without any tact again, "nobody in this wagon train is lending the man any aid nor encouraging him to stay close to us."

Rimmer stiffened in his saddle.

"No, sir. Nobody is, and nobody will. I can promise that."

7

THE GRASS AND SAGEBRUSH grew right down to the river bank.

Fir trees covered the big hill opposite the river. Here and there, a willow grew up along the bank on this side. But by and large it remained a treeless country, at least on the north side of the river. Still, the folks in the wagon train found the valley there at the Bear River near the springs to be a delightful little spot. Not only did they have plenty of water, but the spring water was carbonated, there were hot springs, and the Bear River provided opportunities for fishing and even swimming for those so inclined.

The Townes Party made their camp near one of the springs. The men in the cow column turned the livestock loose in one of the best pieces of grazing ground they'd yet encountered. Thick grass, a wide swath of which was cropped down by preceding livestock, but still plenty to be found within a mile of the worn trail.

They arrived at the valley the previous day around noontime. Rimmer announced they'd reached Beer Springs, and Elias decided to stop for the day. They would spend the afternoon here, and the next day, and leave the following morning. Plenty of time for a respite before going on to Fort Hall.

Late in the day, the wagon train that had been behind them appeared and made their camp. Elias was surprised to realize that train had only been a few hours behind them all this time, but he'd never been aware of their presence so near. The next morning, though, that wagon train broke camp and kept moving and would now be at least a day ahead of them.

Up the trail a piece from where the Townes Party camped, down river maybe two miles, Snake River Indians had made a summer camp. The little village consisted of about a hundred souls, making it just a touch smaller than the group that formed the wagon train. A fair number of those Indians had some English and came down to the camp to trade. The pioneers gave small sacks of flour for blankets. They traded buttons and round shot, both of which were useless to the Natives, for bone necklaces or shirts made of deer skin.

Marcus Weiss boasted to anyone who would listen that he'd traded a brass candle snuffer for a war hammer and a knife made of a black stone that was chipped down to a razor sharp edge. Everyone who saw it had to admit the knife was a real treasure.

Women did laundry in the warm spring and laid shirts out to dry on the sagebrush. Rimmer and his men led a group of almost every man in the party to the "beer" spring where they dipped tin cups into the springwater and tasted for themselves. Some declared it was just sulphur tasting while others said the carbonation did make them feel a bit lightheaded. Others argued that it was the best water they'd had since leaving out of Missouri. A few tasted it and clicked their tongues and announced it did taste exactly like beer.

"I don't taste it," Elias confided to Zeke.

"Nor do I," Zeke said. "But it's an oddity after days of monotony, so I'll gladly take it."

When the men returned to camp with their opinions of the beer spring, the women wanted to find out for themselves. So Rimmer and a few of his men led a second party. Many of the men went with their wives, though some stayed back, complaining that the bubbly water had upset their stomachs.

In the heat of the afternoon, a few of the emigrants napped under canvas covers tied to their wagons and staked to the ground like tents. Several of the men went to one of the springs to bathe. Word spread through the party that Rimmer had suggested making bread from the water, and almost everyone in the party used the water to make bread.

Jeff Pilcher was so delighted by the water from the springs that he got a couple men to help him dump the water from his barrel and they filled it with water from the spring.

Late in the afternoon, as families started to abandon their relaxations for suppertime, Zeke and Marie and their young son Daniel, along with Caleb Driscoll, joined Elias and Maddie at their wagon. More than a dozen of the hands who worked for the Townes brothers and packers and Rimmer and some of his men also joined them. Early in the day, Elias and Zeke and some of the others put a net in the river and managed to get enough fish for a feast. Marie and the Tucker women helped Maddie cook the fish, and they were cooking beans and rice to serve with it, as well as half an ear of corn for everyone.

While the women were still cooking, Elias noticed Stephen Barnes and his wife Gloria wandering away from the wagons, and they seemed to be in some distress.

"I wonder what's going on over there," Elias said.

Zeke and some of the others looked at them.

The Barnes family came from somewhere north of the Ohio. Zeke never could remember if they were from western Indiana or eastern Illinois. Farmers, either way. They kept to themselves, for the most part. Friendly enough with the folks who traveled around them. Always willing to pitch in. Seldom asking for a hand, even when it was evident that they needed one.

Zeke appreciated Stephen and Gloria Barnes.

They had a heap of children. Two older daughters who were just about adults. Maybe fifteen and sixteen, or thereabouts. And three or four younger boys. All of them at an age where they could do something to lend a hand to their ma and pa, and all of them did.

Good folks.

"You sit still," Zeke said to Elias. "I'll go and see if there's a problem."

But Elias was already getting to his feet, and before Zeke could get off the ground, Elias was stomping out across the grass and sage, making for Barnes who was now nearly all the way to the livestock.

They'd let the livestock roam while they camped in the valley, planning to be here a couple of days. Every couple of hours, one of the boys from the cow column would ride around and push back any strays who wandered too far. Most all the steers and goats and milk cows stayed near to each other, though.

"Mr. Barnes!" Elias called and waved his hand, Zeke nearly caught up to him now. "Is something amiss?"

Barnes turned and gave Elias a severe look.

"I'm afraid there might be something, Mr. Townes," Barnes said. His wife Gloria was sixty or seventy yards distant, going one side of the livestock while Barnes made around this way.

"What's the matter?" Elias said.

Still twenty-five or thirty yards separated them and Elias kept walking, even after Barnes started to talk.

"My daughter, Vermilion, she has not returned to our camp."

Vermilion. Zeke remembered, now. The Barnes family came from Vermilion County, Illinois.

"Where was she?" Elias asked.

"She'd gone with my son, Warren. They went to one of the springs, over there." Barnes waved his hand. "Then they came around this large hill. My boy, Warren, he said they were just wandering. And he took a notion to

73

run on ahead. He thought his sister was right behind him. He said he came right through the livestock. And then he joined with his younger brothers who were with me down by the river with our fishing poles."

"How long ago was that?" Elias asked. He and Barnes were face-to-face now, and Zeke stood there with them.

"Mr. Townes, I think it must have been an hour ago. Warren thought his sister must have gone to the wagon to help my wife with the laundry. But no one has seen Vermilion for at least an hour. Maybe more than that."

Elias shot a worried glance at Zeke.

"I'll go and get some of the boys mounted up so we can do a proper search," Zeke said.

"I don't want to be a bother," Barnes said, but the deep lines of worry in his face suggested otherwise.

"It's no bother, Mr. Barnes," Elias said, with a nod at Zeke to go on. "I'll walk with you. Maybe she turned an ankle on the back side of this hill and is just waiting for us to come along and help her."

"I'm sure that's all it is," Barnes said. "You should go back to your supper."

"It'll wait," Elias said.

SEVERAL SPURS OF A low mountain north of the springs reached down toward the Bear River. The spurs created numerous draws and canyons.

The hill where Elias and Stephen Barnes now walked was about a thousand yards long. It was a tall hill, but rounded at the top and with slopes easy enough to walk up. Elias thought he might walk up to the top of the hill and look around to see if he might see the girl. But for now, he walked in the narrow valley between the hill and the nearest mountain spur.

Elias feared they would get around the hill and make for the spring, backtracking the way Warren Barnes had said he'd come, and find the girl floating in a pool of water. For some reason, he had it in his mind that the girl might have drowned.

Whatever happened to her, there was no sign of her in the valley behind the hill.

"I don't understand it," Stephen Barnes said. "She's a responsible girl, Mr. Townes."

"I'm sure that she is," Elias said. "And when we find her, I'm sure she'll have an obvious answer for what delayed her."

Elias purposefully walked out ahead of Barnes. He wanted to get to the spring first, spare the man from seeing something that he might not forget. But when Elias came around the side of the hill, Zeke and Henry Blair were already at the spring, mounted on their horses. Zeke had a couple of his dogs with him. When he saw Elias from a distance, Zeke turned Duke in his brother's direction and whistled at the dogs.

"No sign of her around the spring," Zeke said. "Some of the others are getting their horses, but we're going to run out of daylight soon."

Elias nodded his head, and Zeke could see the strain on his face.

"What are your thoughts, brother?"

Elias glanced back to find Stephen Barnes. He was still some distance off, having walked up to look around at the foot of one of the mountain spurs.

"My thoughts are we're going to run out of daylight soon. Would you ride over to that Indian village? Ask if they've seen a girl?"

Zeke clicked his tongue and glanced to the west in the direction of the village. He'd had an encounter with some Snake braves back at the South Pass, and he wasn't eager to have another encounter with a band of Indians. But these folks had been pleasant enough, coming to trade with the pioneers, and they had some English. Clearly, they'd been camped here along the Bear River all summer, and they'd encountered plenty of other white men in wagon trains.

"I'll do that," Zeke said.

"Take Henry with you," Elias said. "If they give you any trouble, just ride back here fast as you can."

Zeke rode out to the west, toward the Indian village, with his dogs and Henry Blair following behind, and Elias turned back to Barnes.

The man kept a stoic countenance, but his behavior became more hurried. He rushed to look behind any rock large enough for a young woman to hide behind. He walked part way up the big hillside, but then turned around and walked back down it again.

By now numerous men from the wagon train were out walking around in the valley, many of them toting sticks. Several had gone down to the riverbank and were searching there. Some of the women had gone to Gloria Barnes and brought her back to the camp and were trying to reassure her. Other mothers quickly counted their children to make certain all were accounted for.

Meanwhile, the sun got ever lower on the western horizon.

At dawn, the Townes Party resumed its search for Vermilion Barnes.

Elias had intended to break camp and get moving, but the disappearance of the girl altered those plans.

Many among the party had spent a sleepless night, wandering some distance from the camp in hopes of perhaps hearing the girl call for help. Several times in the night, Gloria Barnes walked out away from the camp and called for her daughter – her funereal calls settling a somber mood among the emigrants.

"I think you should consider moving on," Neil Rimmer said to Elias just before the sun's rays spread across the eastern horizon.

"Not while the girl is missing," Elias answered him.

Rimmer nodded his head and gave his shoulders a small shrug.

"You paid me to guide you. That's my guidance. But it's your decision to make."

"We've got to make some effort to find the girl," Elias said.

"Probably toted off by savages," Rimmer said. "It happens, you know. A girl wanders off by herself, out of sight, Indians take her. They'll adopt her into their tribe, marry her to a chief or something."

But Elias didn't think so. The Indians in the village up the trail, they'd been nothing but peaceful. And there'd been no other signs of Indians. Elias was certain that if Indians mounted on ponies had snatched Vermilion Barnes, there would have been tracks. But he saw nothing to indicate hostiles nearby.

"What happened to your face, Mr. Rimmer?" Elias asked, noticing as Rimmer turned so that the early morning light caught the side of his face, that he had a bad scratch going from his cheek down to his neck.

Rimmer chuckled and touched his hand to the scratch on the side of his face.

"Fell in some brush down by the spring yesterday. Squatting down to fill my cup and lost my footing. Lucky I didn't go right into the water." Then he went back to the subject concerning him. "You saw yesterday that some of these peaks still have snow on them?"

"I did," Elias admitted. He'd noticed it all through the Bear River Valley. Distant mountain peaks patched in white. "It's July, the heat of summer, but you can still see snow. I know in Kentucky you've never seen nothing like that. What I'm saying to you, Mr. Townes, it seems like snow is the last thing we have to worry about. But a wagon wheel busts and we lose a day. The river is flooding when we go to cross the Snake and we lose maybe a week. We'll delay at least a little while at Fort Hall. Maybe somewhere along the line the livestock stampedes and we lose a few days trying to round them all back up. Add in all those delays to the time that it takes if we don't have any problems – not a single delay – and you're looking at snow in the Blue Mountains. You want to see half these people dead by December? Get caught in the Blue Mountains in the snow. You won't be mourning one girl that got carried off by Injuns. You'll be mourning all these folks that trusted you to get them to Oregon City."

Elias swallowed hard and nodded his head.

"One more day, Mr. Rimmer. One more day of looking, and tomorrow we'll move."

The morning's search was more organized by far than the search in the previous afternoon.

Elias sent several of the mounted men up the nearest spurs of the mountain. No one could say why the girl might have wandered up into the high ground, but unless she'd fallen into the river and been swept downstream, the mountain spurs were the only option where she might have disappeared. Perhaps she'd wrong footed on a steep drop and suffered through the night with a broken leg or turned ankle.

It was possible, Elias knew, that a cat or wolf or even a bear might have gotten her and dragged her up into the high places. He'd seen no animal sign to suggest such a fate, but the ground was dry and grassy and hard, and an animal might not have left obvious tracks.

There was also a long draw that reached deep between two spurs, growing narrower into a canyon as it went. Many crooks and crannies, easy places for a person to have gotten hurt climbing up a rock face.

The Indians at the village downriver had told Zeke they didn't see the girl, and Zeke said they had women doing laundry and men fishing throughout the day. Nevertheless, Elias sent some of the men on horseback downstream. The most logical thing to him was that the girl had fallen in the river, drowned, and her body swept away. How else could she have just disappeared? The current wasn't so swift, but if she was weighted down by her dress and couldn't come up for air, it certainly could have carried her some distance down the river.

The sun rose behind them, breaking free of the heights behind them.

Elias went behind the hill again, the last place Vermilion had been seen, and searched for tracks or animal sign a while longer.

Some of the men he'd sent out on horseback returned around noon, reporting they'd seen nothing of her.

The men he'd sent down river came back later in the afternoon. They'd gone several miles down the river.

"Up ahead, the river curves around a mountain spur and then drops south," Jeff Pilcher told him. "If she'd fallen into the river, I am confident her body would have hung up at the bend. But we went on probably another five miles or so. Nothing."

The celebratory mood of the previous two days was gone. Not a soul at the camp didn't have thoughts of Vermilion Barnes or her distraught mother and father.

It struck Elias that this wagon train had become so much like an extended family. Most of them now had been weeks together, the entire world shrunk down to the mile or two of trail that their wagon train occupied at any given time.

Reverend Marsh spent time with Gloria Barnes, praying with her. Older children from other families went to take care of the younger Barnes children and to console Isabel, the older daughter.

It might have been another serene day, pleasantly spent in this lovely valley. Children might have frolicked down by the river or in the open, grassy fields. Perhaps the men would have gone shooting or tried to hunt game in the canyons, or fished. Maybe the women would have made more bread or rested from the previous day's labors with the laundry.

But for the Townes Party, the extra day at the Bear River valley near the Beer Springs turned out to be one of anxious dread. And as it neared its end, it became a day they would all remember for its sorrow.

It was Henry Blair who found Vermilion Barnes.

8

THE LONG CANYON STRETCHED back more than a mile. Maybe it was two miles. It was narrow with high rocky walls, formed by two long spurs from the mountain. It ended in a gently rising draw that stretched up to the long ridge of one of those spurs.

Zeke and Henry had ridden together through the canyon earlier in the day. They'd gone up the draw and come out on the ridge where other men who'd approached the ridge from a different side were already searching. They rode down a different way and came at the camp from the northeast.

Still no sign of the girl.

"Let's ride through that canyon again," Zeke proposed.

"We checked it pretty thoroughly," Henry said.

"I know we did, but it's better than sitting here waiting."

So Henry agreed.

A number of draws ran up the sides of the spurs along the length of the canyon. Some narrow and steep. Others wider, gentler slopes. Juniper clung to the sides of the hills, in some places so thick they couldn't hardly see through it.

Now, Zeke and Henry rode into each of those draws, looked around and rode back out. In most cases it was unnecessary. If the girl had been in any of those draws, they'd have seen her. But some of them, littered with juniper, Henry conceded that maybe it was worthwhile to look about some.

They were maybe a mile into the canyon when Zeke pointed to a ridgeline partway up the spur to their left.

"Can you make it up there, Henry?" Zeke asked.

Henry judged it.

"Not on horseback," he said. "But I can walk it."

"Go and have a look," Zeke suggested.

Henry dropped down out of his saddle and handed his reins over to Zeke who was taking a drink of water from his canteen.

It was a rocky, difficult trail up to that ridge. Steep enough in some places that Henry was having to pull himself up with his hands.

"I don't hardly think she'd have come this way," Henry called back under his armpit, pulling himself up higher.

"Well, since she ain't come back yet, a way we think she wouldn't have gone will probably be where we find her."

Henry sighed and heaved himself up, planted a knee and pushed himself upright. He nearly fell back at the shock of seeing what looked like a pile of clothes hidden down beneath a juniper. But then Henry realized the pile of clothes had the bare legs of a young woman sticking out of them.

"Mr. Zeke," Henry called, unable to take his eyes from the sight. "You'd better come up here."

Zeke Townes moved fast. A young man, athletic and agile in spite of his big frame, and Henry felt embarrassed at how quickly Zeke was standing beside him. But he stood beside Henry for just a moment. Then he was beside the woman's body. Her dress had been pulled up over her head and arms, and that's why Henry at first thought she was just a pile of clothes. But Zeke lifted up the dress and saw that it was Vermilion Barnes. Though he could hardly tell, even upon seeing her face.

"Dammit all to hell," Zeke muttered under his breath.

"Is that her?" Henry said.

Henry couldn't see from where he stood, Zeke squatting down between him and the girl, and Zeke didn't pull the dress fully away from her head.

She'd been scalped and her throat was cut. Her eyes stared deathly horror at him. As he looked around, Zeke could see her undergarments pushed into the juniper bush where they wouldn't blow away or be easily seen. She'd been violated and murdered, the corpse defiled. The poor girl had gone through a brutal final minutes, however long it had lasted.

"Henry, climb back down there and go get my brother. Tell him we found the girl. Do it in a subtle way so as not to cause alarm. Tell Elias, maybe it would be best not to bring her father."

"You've gone pale, Mr. Zeke. What is it?"

"She's in a bad condition, Henry," was all Zeke would say.

Henry scrambled back down the trail, and Zeke looked around while he waited for Henry to return with Elias.

There were clear tracks on the ground here that suggested maybe Vermilion had put up a fight. Marks in the dirt where a boot skidded, where a body slid across the dirt. Zeke could find dried blood on the dirt, too. Blood on a big rock, blood soaking into the dress. Vermilion Barnes had undergone a brutal attack up here.

She'd not been dragged up to the ridge. She'd either been coaxed or threatened up here. Nobody carried her up or dragged her.

The attack had come here on the ridge. They'd been out of sight of the wagons, far enough away that no one would have heard the struggle.

Zeke had longer up on that ridge than he'd wanted, but eventually he saw Henry Blair returning with Elias and some other men riding behind. Zeke took a breath when he saw that Stephen Barnes was among them.

As the sun set, they buried Vermilion Barnes on the hill overlooking the river and the camp. Stephen Barnes said that the body wouldn't wash away if the river flooded.

Barnes and his wife and children and several of the other emigrants from the Townes Party climbed the hill. They'd wrapped the body in linens. Nobody wanted for Gloria Barnes to see her daughter's mutilated corpse.

Already a whisper circled the camp.

"Who do you think could've done it?" Jeff Pilcher asked Zeke. "Most everyone I've talked to thinks it must've been an Injun, seeing as how she was scalped."

Zeke shook his head.

"I don't know, Jeff," Zeke said.

But he had an idea who had done it. Those who attended the funeral were now just getting to their supper, Zeke included. He couldn't remember the last time he'd had anything to eat. His supper the day before had been interrupted, and he'd set out as sunup to look for this girl this morning.

Marie gave him a plate of food and he ate quietly by himself. She'd already fed Caleb Driscoll and Daniel and herself. The sun had dropped below the western horizon but still gave light to the evening sky, light enough that Marie could see Elias walking along the outside of the wagons.

"Your brother's coming," Marie said, a look of aggravation flashing across her face.

"Uh-huh," Zeke said. "I ain't surprised. He's thinking the same thing I'm thinking."

"And what is that?"

"That man Norwood, who was with Rimmer? He's likely the man that done this to the Barnes girl."

"And what is he going to want to do about it?" Marie asked, but she didn't need to ask. She knew as well as Zeke did.

Zeke glanced in the direction that Elias was coming. Saw him there with his holstered saddle gun on his hip, a rifle in his hand, a big fighting knife sheathed on his belt.

"I expect he's going to want to go and find Mr. Norwood," Zeke said.

Marie gave her husband a stern look.

"Not until you've finished your supper."

Beans and rice. Zeke scooped another bite into his mouth, sitting on a cracker box and holding his plate in his hand.

"Yes, ma'am," he said through a full mouth. "I'll eat first."

Zeke managed two more bites, and was still chewing when Elias got to their wagon.

"You just about finished there?" Elias asked.

"I will be in momentarily," Zeke said.

"We're going to find Norwood."

"I figured."

"I don't want to get a big group together. Just a few folks."

Caleb Driscoll, sitting nearby, volunteered.

"You'll stay here," Zeke said. "Somebody's got to keep a watch on my wagon while I'm gone."

Captain Walker made his way over to them, his cavalry sword on his belt and a rifle in hand. And Henry Blair walked with him. Zeke knew that Henry was compelled to join Elias's posse from the shock of finding the girl. But to Zeke's surprise, Stephen Barnes also walked with them.

"You sure it's wise to bring the girl's father?" Zeke muttered to Elias.

But Elias answered him with a shrug.

"It's his right. He was her father."

Zeke nodded his head. He scooped in another bite, hurrying now. He was famished, but he knew these men wouldn't wait long.

When he finished, Zeke went to the wagon with a lantern and got his Colt Paterson, a Number 5 Holster Gun. Elias bought himself and Zeke matching revolvers for making this trip. He also got them matching Leman percussion rifles, and with a knife tucked into his belt, Zeke made himself identically armed to his brother.

The last bit of gray light of day fell around them now. It would be dark soon, but the moon already hung in the eastern sky.

Captain Walker saddled his horse and Stephen Barnes took a horse from Elias's remuda, not having a saddle horse of his own. Zeke saddled Duke, and Elias saddled Tuckee. Henry got his horse, and shortly they were ready to go and hunt for Norwood.

Elias led the small company of men away from the wagons, and they'd not gone far when the figure of two mounted men appeared coming from the wagons, and one of them called out to Elias.

"Mr. Townes?"

"Is that you, Mr. Rimmer?" Elias said, turning and squinting into the silvery light cast by the moon.

Now Rimmer was catching up, and Elias could see him more clearly.

"I reckon you're going to look for Norwood?" Rimmer said.

"I should have dealt with him when we first noticed him nearby."

"Maybe so," Rimmer said. "If you don't mind, me and Bowden would like to come along to look for him."

Elias did not answer for several moments.

"I don't want you to be in an awkward position, Mr. Rimmer," Elias said at last. "You've told me Norwood was not a friend, that your association with him was purely from necessity. Nevertheless, you did have an association with him. If we have a confrontation with the man, it might be best for you not to be involved."

Rimmer chuckled.

"If you're worried about whether or not I'll gut him with my knife, Mr. Townes, you needn't. I'll cut the man if he makes us cut him."

Elias groaned.

"Besides," Rimmer continued. "I know him a mite, and maybe me and Bowden can scare him up."

"All right," Elias said. "I suppose you can come along."

Now the small posse turned and started out across the fields, and Elias spoke close to Zeke's shoulder in a whisper.

"Keep a watch on those two men," he said.

ELIAS HAD HOPED TO make a quick job of this, but they'd seen nothing of Norwood since they'd come over the top of the mountain spur and had to bury Noah Bloom. They did not know for sure that he was even still behind them. It was possible he might have joined up with that other party. Though it was doubtful they'd not recognize him, considering it was one of their number who Norwood had stolen money from back at Bridger's Fort.

They rode out maybe five miles back down the trail. They had to hope to see a campfire or at least smell smoke. They checked some of the springs and creeks, but found no sign of Norwood.

Sometime in the early morning hours, when they'd turned back and were making for the wagons, Rimmer suggested another spot.

"There's a spring to the north, off the trail a couple of miles," he said. "It's on the eastern side of them spurs we camped near, probably about five miles from the wagons. But like I said, there's a spring up that away. Nobody comes by that spring. Too far off the trail. Emigrants all stop at the springs nearer to the river. But we've camped up there. A few willow trees around it, nice shade. A little stream coming from the spring. It's a good spot, and Norwood knows it."

They spread out some, the seven of them, reasoning that in the moonlight a group of people gathered together might be more apt to attract attention whereas single riders spread out might go unnoticed.

The spring sat down near the base of a hill, and within a mile or so of it, Rimmer made his way over to Elias. He suggested a couple of them should swing around behind the spring, just in case Norwood saw them coming and tried to make a run. Elias sent Captain Walker with Henry Blair and Stephen Barnes.

They waited a while, giving the others time to swing wide and get in behind the spring, marked by a stand of short willows and a larger cottonwood or two that showed black in the silvery light.

While the others went wide to get in behind the spring, Rimmer went alone, getting within a couple hundred yards of the spring. Then he made his way back to Elias, Zeke, and the man called Bowden.

"He's up there," Rimmer said. "Or he has been recently. I didn't dare get too close. I don't want to spook his horse. But I can smell smoke. He had a fire burning not long ago. Probably still smoldering."

"We'll give them a few more minutes to get in place," Elias said. "When we go, I want to move fast. But I want to grab him alive. It's not my intention to kill an innocent man."

"How are you going to know if he's an innocent man or not?" Rimmer said.

"Whoever killed Vermilion Barnes took her scalp," Elias said. "If he has the scalp, we'll know."

"What if he threw it out?" Rimmer asked.

"What's the point of taking it if he's just going to throw it out?" Elias asked. "If he did it, he'll still have it."

"He might also confess," Zeke said. "If he's caught, he might confess."

"He won't do that," Rimmer said doubtfully. "But maybe he has that scalp."

When they decided the other had time enough to swing around the spring, Zeke noted that a gray light showed in the sky. Dawn was coming on them. In a matter of less than an hour it would be light enough to see more than silvery shadows.

"Let's move toward the spring," Elias said. "Everyone be on guard. If we see movement or hear a horse alert to us or anything unnatural, don't wait for an order. Charge the spring. Bring Norwood under control."

The night was plenty cool, but Zeke felt sweat beading at the edge of his hat and on his back.

He gave a touch to Duke's shoulder and moved the horse wide so that if Norwood tried to run maybe he'd be able to charge him and drag him down. Zeke felt a responsibility to be first into the action to keep his brother safe. All these souls depended on Elias to return. They'd get to Oregon City even if Zeke did not.

They walked their horses. Slow and easy. The light in the sky grew a touch brighter. Zeke could look out across the wide prairie and see the other three riders with him. They were spread out with twenty or so yards between each one. Elias was there on the farthest side.

Within a couple hundred yards, Zeke could smell smoke. Then he saw movement down under one of the willow trees, and he was all but certain it was a horse or mule he'd seen there.

And then he heard from the stand of trees a horse blow. Zeke knew as well as anyone that a man sleeping along in this enormous wilderness would sleep lightly, and a blow or a snort or a tap on the ground from a horse's hoof would be enough to bring him awake and reaching for his gun. Zeke didn't wait.

Duke felt the pent tension release, and without bidding the horse bounded forward. Zeke felt like a cavalryman at the charge. The horse cleared ten yards, then thirty. Zeke reached down with his right and felt the grip of the Paterson revolver there. Seventy yards. Zeke moved with the horse, controlling the movement of his body in his hips. He tried to make himself light so that Duke could fly easily over the land.

Half the distance gone.

Zeke saw more movement now under the willows there by the spring. He knew there was a stream up ahead, but not exactly sure where. His eyes searched the ground for a curled line of black. He'd never seen the stream here before, but somehow he sensed it. Shallow and narrow coming from a single spring. Curves like dropped length of string. It would show black as the first light of day cast a gray pall over the landscape. Black where no light had yet reached.

A hundred and thirty yards gone. He'd be on the stand of trees in seventy yards or fewer.

There! The depression in the earth curling down toward Bear Creek. Not two feet wide. Duke jumped it, just as Zeke saw a dark shadow break loose from the stand of trees and run into the wide field. A single man on foot, running in the night to try to save his life.

Duke didn't have to be directed. Zeke's eyes locked on the man, and the horse bounded toward him. They'd be on him in twenty yards.

Zeke slid a foot free from the stirrup and stuck out his leg just as they came on the man. Zeke gave him a wallop in the head, one that bruises his own shin. The man went down in a heap and Zeke now pulled the reins, turning the horse.

He dropped down from the saddle and drew out the saddle gun from its holster on his hip.

Zeke didn't even draw back the hammer to release the embedded trigger. Instead, he gripped the revolver stiffly and gave it a back-handed swing. The heavy barrel smashed the man in the side of the head as he tried to push himself up from his hands and knees. Now the man fell back down with a yelp.

Zeke thumbed back the hammer on the saddle gun. Felt the trigger drop down and put his index finger against it.

"Give me any excuse to blast a hole the size of Missouri into you," Zeke said.

"MR. NORWOOD," ELIAS SAID, standing over the man. "We've come for you because of the girl."

"What girl?" Norwood asked.

He'd had a bag slung over his shoulder when he was running, and Zeke picked it up now. He pulled loose the knot in the drawstrings and loosened the top.

Rimmer and Bowden were there with Elias, the three of them standing over Norwood.

Zeke felt a knife, some powder and shot, a small sack of flour in the bag. A shirt was in there. He pulled some of these things out of the bag as he searched it. What he did not find was the scalp of a teenage girl.

"You tell us what happened," Elias said. "How did you come upon her? What made you do it?"

"Do what?" Norwood asked. The man sounded scared.

"Get him to his feet," Zeke said. "Disarm the man so he don't gut one of us and think to run."

"I don't know what you're talking about," Norwood said. "I admit I've been following you, but that's all. I haven't done nothing else to molest your party. Not one thing!"

"We should go and check his camp," Zeke said, and he gave the bag a shake. "I don't think what we're looking for is in here."

"Tell me what you're talking about!" Norwood shouted, sounding more desperate and scared by the moment.

Elias and Bowden jerked him to his feet, and in the grayness, Zeke could see that the side of his head was bleeding from the blow he'd taken from the barrel of Zeke's Paterson.

"The girl you murdered," Zeke said, coming around to face Norwood.

Rimmer took the bag from Zeke as Zeke reached out and plucked a knife from Norwood's belt. As far as he could see, the knife was the only weapon Norwood had on him. All the same, Zeke patted the sides of the man's shirt just to be sure there wasn't some other implement hidden there. He noticed, too, three figures on foot and leading horses toward them, coming from the back side of the spring. Captain Walker, Henry Blair, and Stephen Barnes.

"I don't know what you're talking about," Norwood said. "I admit, I've been following you. But just to keep myself safe from Indian attack. Tell them, Rimmer. I don't mean no harm."

Rimmer held Norwood's bag in one hand, the other reaching inside, feeling around. He glanced up at Norwood.

"If you did something with that girl, you best just go on and confess it," Rimmer said.

"I don't know nothing about a girl," Norwood pleaded.

Captain Walker and the others were up to the group now. Barnes walked around to the side of his horse.

"Is this the man?" Barnes asked. "The man who killed my daughter?"

Norwood's eyes grew wide and he looked at Elias.

"I didn't kill nobody."

"Hang on, now," Rimmer said. "What in the hell is this?"

He plucked something from Norwood's bag. Even in the dim light, nobody had to question what it was. The strands of hair fell long from the sickening bit of skin and flesh.

"I didn't –" Norwood started, but his words of denial were cut short by the flash and blast of Stephen Barnes's rifle.

All of the men jerked and ducked or stepped clear. The thunderous bark of the gun caught them all by surprise, but none more than Norwood himself, who was not only caught by the thunderous bark but also by the ball of lead that burst forth from the barrel. The lead ball smashed into Norwood's chest, and the man's body seemed to suspend their on its legs for just a second before collapsing to the ground.

Norwood choked and spit. His eyes glowed blue in the gray light. His face dirty and bearded. His mouth hanging open as he gasped for breath.

"I'd have liked to been able to kill you a thousand times over," Barnes said, walking calmly forward and standing over the body. "I'd have liked to been able to start off ever day for the rest of my life by shooting and killing you, again and again and again. But this one time will have to do. You're a vile man, and may my vengeance be nothing compared to what God does to you."

Norwood didn't move. He'd collapsed on his back, and though he choked for breath and blood spurted from his mouth and his eyes stared fearfully at the gray sky above, he didn't move. He lingered there for several minutes, and Zeke worried that he wasn't going to die straight away. What would they do with him if he held on for a few days?

As it was, the group of seven emigrants stood for several minutes in a circle over the dying man. Nobody spoke. Nobody offered comfort in any way to the dying. None of them felt any compassion toward the man.

At last, the gasping and choking turned to rattling and gurgling, and then the breaths came no more and Norwood stared blankly.

"We should bury him," Elias said.

"Strip him and leave him for the coyotes," Barnes said. "That's what he intended for my daughter."

Elias released a heavy breath.

"Captain Walker? Would you take Mr. Barnes back to camp?"

Walker nodded, took Barnes by the arm, and Barnes did not resist.

"What should I do with this?" Rimmer asked, holding Vermilion Barnes's stolen scalp and long locks of hair between his fingers.

"Never let me see that again," Barnes said.

9

MUSTARD WENT TO WORK on the side of his head with his back paw, scratching at it like he was trying to kick his own head off.

Daniel laughed, but then remembered his own bites and went to scratching his arm. Marie testily snatched at the buzzing near her ear, checked her hand and realized immediately she'd been unsuccessful when the buzzing returned. Now she slapped the side of her head.

"It's misery," she said.

"I thought the mosquitoes at home coming up off the Ohio River were unmerciful, but I've never seen anything like this," Zeke said, waving an arm in front of him in a futile effort to bat some of them away. Zeke watched his wife slap at a mosquito on her arm.

"Got him!" she said, picking the smashed bug off her arm.

"Do you regret coming, now? Molested by mosquitoes and fifteen hundred miles on your feet. Barren landscape the whole way. Do you wish we'd stayed at home?"

Marie smiled, her hazel eyes bright and full of love. She shook her head.

"I do not regret it at all," she said. "Nor do I think the landscape is terribly barren. It's beautiful, all of it. All part of God's wonderful creation. In fact, every time I see a hill on the horizon, I get excited because I cannot wait to see what it beyond that hill. I want to see it all. Every tree and rock and river. It's all so big and beautiful. I never knew – I never imagined in all my life – that the world could be so big!"

Zeke smiled at her. He'd always loved her, even before he was old enough to know what that meant. Back when she was just his best friend and they played in the fields and swam the swimming holes together. But he felt now, seeing how she cheerfully accepted the hardships of this journey, that he'd found new appreciation for this woman.

"It won't get easier," Zeke said. "And even when we get where we're going, who knows what we'll find there? It could be a hard winter."

"We'll get through the hardship together," Marie said. "We're doing this to build a better life. We're doing this to reach for something bigger. But I never expected getting there would be easy. If it was easy, there would be a lot more wagons on this trail with us."

The party camped near the old Hudson Bay Company fort that they'd reached the previous day. They'd made the seventy miles from Beer Spring in four days. The man in charge at Fort Hall, Captain Grant, had offered fresh milk to whoever wanted it. The children among the Townes Party readily accepted, as did most of the women and some of the men. There was a modest amount of whiskey for sale by the gallon. He had onions and lettuce that he gave away at no charge. But the fort offered nothing else in the way of provisions for sale or trade.

They had left the Bear River just beyond the spot where they'd buried Vermilion Barnes. The river there made a severe bend and dropped south. But the Townes Party had continued on north and west, following the Portneuf River for most of the seventy miles remaining to Fort Hall. It should have been a two-week journey from Bridger's Fort to Fort Hall, even allowing for a day or two of rest at the springs. Instead, they'd taken twenty days to reach the white adobe walls of Fort Hall.

The last few miles of trail had been hilly countryside, rocky and difficult ground. The wagons lurched and bounced so that even the most weary of the emigrants among them chose to walk rather than have their brains rattled and their guts jarred. The promise of arriving soon at Fort Hall had filled Zeke and many of the others with a bit of hope – if for nothing else, for the opportunity to rest a bit. But the ground between Fort Hall and the Snake River was cut with little streams and creeks, as marshy a ground as they'd seen in some time, and so filled with mosquitoes that the hoped for rest proved worse than the hilly ground.

"I've been here about three years," Grant said. "Long enough that I've seen a lot of folks come through. The road to California breaks away from the road to Oregon just west of here, and if you're planning to make for California, I'd advise you to leave your wagons where they stand," Grant told them. "Pack from here."

"We're bound for Oregon City," Elias told him.

Grant twisted his lips into a look of dreaded consternation.

"Might want to leave those wagons anyway," he said.

"It's rough travel from here, folks. It's a bad road from here to Oregon City. You've got rivers to cross and mountains to scale. Be a mite easier on you folks if you was all mounted and not trying to pull these wagons."

Elias thanked him for the information but did not take it seriously. Others in the party, though, did begin to talk seriously of abandoning their wagons.

Rimmer advised against it.

"It'll be tough going. We'll have some hills to go down that are worse than that one we had to descend over on the Bear River. But we can manage it. We've got plenty of strong men. I'm more worried about snow than I am wagons. This wagon train has to keep moving."

So they did not linger at Fort Hall.

The next morning the wagons rolled out, and no one particularly felt sad to bid farewell to the mosquitoes.

They made the better part of twenty miles. Hilly countryside, but the Snake River always off their right shoulders.

At the fort there'd been a ceaseless parade of Shoshone – the Snake River People – coming and going. They came in twos or threes or by dozens or scores. Now, out on the open prairie, Indians became a common sight. Some, who had some English, would come up to the wagon train, seeking to make a trade. A bit of bread or some rice could get a pair of moccasins. Jeff Pilcher traded a shirt for what he took to be fresh elk meat, though he and the Snake Indian he got the meat from had such a language barrier that Jeff never could be sure what his family had for supper that night. He said it tasted a little sweet, so he thought maybe it was antelope.

Several of the people in the party took ill on that second day, and Elias feared they might be delayed many more days.

The company camped at a wide falls in the river, a spot not more than five or six miles from where they'd camped the previous night.

Those not sick walked down to admire the falls, and to be away from the camp full of those who were sick. The falls themselves were wide with a great expanse of rock jutting out in the middle and dividing the falls into two separate streams. For those who'd escaped illness, the falls proved to be a memorable attraction. They roared loud through the camp, and those who went to the bank to see them had to shout to be overheard. For Elias, though, the beauty of the falls only served to mark a day of lost travel.

Rimmer surmised it was the mosquitoes back at Fort Hall that made everyone so sick.

While most of the folks had only a small case of what ailed them, Reverend Marsh took ill in a bad way. He became delirious with a fever overnight and at one point had to be physically restrained to keep him from wandering toward the river.

"I need a drink of water!" he'd shouted several times as two or three men held him back and finally got him to lie back down in his bedroll.

"You must hold the wagon train," Lillian Marsh told Elias the next morning as the wagons were preparing to start out for the day. "Reverend Marsh is unable to leave this morning."

"Can he not ride a horse?" Elias asked. "If it's only an issue of securing a driver for you, I can find someone to drive your team."

"I assure you, Mr. Townes, he cannot ride a horse in his condition."

"Perhaps, then, he can ride in the wagon," Elias said.

Rimmer was there, and Zeke and a few others, all hearing the pastor's wife make her demand to hold the wagon train another day.

"I'm afraid he is in such a state that riding in the wagon would be equally impossible. I am sure if you could wait just one more day he would be fit to go in the morning."

Elias let out a slow and heavy breath. He gave a glance to Zeke who merely shrugged his shoulders helplessly.

"We cannot delay this wagon train unnecessarily," Rimmer said. "I'm serious when I tell you that you don't understand how fast winter can come and how bad it might be. I've been up in this very part of the country at wintertime before. I wintered one time there at Fort Hall where we just left. I can tell you there were snow drifts down in the low places that were twenty feet deep that winter. If we don't keep this wagon train rolling, we're going to be fighting the snow. Look around you, Mr. Townes."

Indeed, for the third morning of the last five, there was a light frost on the ground. Still July, and frost on the ground. On the mountaintops in the distance, large patches of snow could be seen.

Elias knew July and August as hot months. Sultry, uncomfortable, hot months. Humid down by the Ohio River. He knew that frost on the ground was proof that this was a different countryside, one that he still knew little about. He had to rely on the advice of a man who knew this place.

"We need to keep moving," Rimmer declared.

"Ma'am, I can give you whatever aid you require to keep your wagon going," Elias said. "We've got plenty of men here who can help you. But Reverend Marsh is going to have to be able to ride or walk. He's going to have to move out with us." Elias paused in his speech. Time enough to take a breath before uttering the words he did not want to say. "Or we'll have to leave you behind."

"Mr. Townes!" Lillian Marsh gasped. "You cannot."

Elias took a breath.

"Ma'am, I wouldn't want to, but I've got to get these people safely to Oregon City. If you're husband cannot travel, then perhaps your best option is to camp here for another day or two and then turn back to Fort Hall. The fort sits less than thirty miles from here. You could winter there at the fort and move on to the Oregon Territory in the spring."

"My husband is going to the Northwest Territory to serve as a missionary to the native peoples," Lillian Marsh said, squaring her shoulders. "He is going to do the Lord's work, Mr. Townes. Surely, your wagon train can wait one more day for a man who intends to serve the Lord."

Zeke watched the consternation on Elias's face with some amusement, glad that he did not stand in his brother's shoes at the moment.

"Maybe I can offer a solution," Rimmer interrupted, with a glance at Lillian Marsh. "I could leave two of my men back with the preacher and his wife. Henry Temple and one of the others. We can get the rest of these wagons moving, and when the preacher is feeling up to it – tomorrow or even the next day – Henry could get them going. I believe Temple and another man moving just one wagon could catch up to the main body of the wagon train in three days. Maybe two. Hell, if they leave out in the morning, they might catch us tomorrow afternoon. You can move one wagon a lot faster than you can move a whole train of wagons."

Elias considered it for a moment.

He toed some of the grass with the dusting of frost. He glanced to the east at the sun slowly breaking the horizon.

"Mrs. Marsh, is that amenable to you?"

Lillian Marsh's face was stern and rigid. Clearly, she didn't like the option. She kept her lips pursed. Her husband was on the mend. His fever had broken, but he was asleep now and probably still too ill to participate in the discussion. Zeke, watching her, could see how indecisive she felt. The woman wanted the entire wagon train to wait, and probably because that would alleviate her having to make this decision.

"I suppose we have little choice," Lillian Marsh said. "We cannot turn back for the fort. There are souls to save, Mr. Townes. And if you will not wait on us, then our only option is to accept the help of these men and press forward with haste when Reverend Marsh is fit. Now I will go and see to my husband."

Lillian Marsh left them, and most of the others who were standing there also left. Work to do. Teams to hitch. Gear to stow.

"This man, Temple?" Elias said. "He's trustworthy?"

"Of course he is," Rimmer said.

"I mean, competent. Is he competent to get the Marsh wagon caught back up to us?"

"He's competent as hell," Rimmer said. "He's been out here forever. He's an H.B.C. man, Mr. Townes."

"Hudson Bay Company?" Townes said.

Rimmer answered with a chuckle at his own joke.

"No sir. Here before Christ."

10

MARIE RODE HER BROWN and white pinto pony up to the hill where Duke stood. Zeke sat his saddle Daniel nestled in front of him, the boy's head alternating between lolling forward and resting against Zeke's chest.

The Snake River, easily a thousand feet wide here, with an island right in the middle, moved lazily down below. The river cut a canyon with sharp banks, especially on the far side where the escarpments in places dropped thirty vertical feet down to the water. But in other places, the bank was easy enough that they could walk the livestock right down to the river to water them.

For now, the wagons moved through a large rock garden. The path clear enough, but the rocks forcing the emigrants through a narrow channel.

"Lazily," Zeke said out loud.

"What's that?" Marie asked.

"I was just thinking that the river is moving lazily, but that's not really true. That current is swift."

He pointed to the ripples on the surface that showed the water's movement.

"Do we cross this river?" Marie asked.

"We do. Two or three times, I don't remember. But we don't cross it until farther on, and I know one of the crossings is broken by islands."

"It seems enormous," Marie said. "How deep is it?"

"I would imagine pretty deep," Zeke said, though he wasn't even sure what that meant. "Maybe ten feet or fifteen."

The water was a dark gray, almost black, suggesting it ran pretty deep. Certainly plenty deep to make any crossing treacherous. But what worried Zeke more was the swiftness of the water. It looked like an easy rolling river, but a man who knew rivers could plainly see the curl of the undercurrent.

Half as wide as the Mississippi or the Ohio. About the same size as the Missouri.

But they'd ferried over those rivers. They'd forded the Platte, back-breaking work for the oxen as they dragged the wagons through the sandy bottom. They'd even used long rope to hitch teams on dry land to help the oxen trudging through the sandy bottom of the Platte. At the Sweetwater and other smaller rivers and creeks, the Townes Party had also forded those rivers. Some had been as easy as pulling the wagons across dry land. Others more of a chore. But so far, they'd been fortunate to cross with none of the rivers flooding. The only severe mishap on a river had been an overturned wagon on the Missouri ferry. A family forced to abandon their plans of a westward journey, at least for 1846. Zeke figured they'd try it again the next year, but maybe not.

The Snake would be their first time having to cross a swift current floating their wagons and swimming the livestock. If they only lost a quarter of their livestock, the could count themselves lucky. But how many people would they lose? The question tied Zeke's stomach in a knot, and he couldn't imagine how much it weighed on Elias.

"How soon before we have to cross it?" Marie asked.

It was Rimmer who provided the answer, riding up to them just as Marie asked the question.

"Ma'am, we won't cross the Snake for another two hundred miles or so," Rimmer said with a nod to Zeke. "We'll have to get across the Raft River first, and I expect that'll be tomorrow. It'll be a job, I can tell you that."

"The Raft River?" Zeke said. "I don't remember that on the brochure."

Rimmer grinned at him. Cocked his head and looked sideways.

"Brochure?" Rimmer asked.

"My brother has a brochure. It's a guide to the trail. All the landmarks are noted. The river crossings. The points of interest."

Rimmer chuckled.

"Well, I ain't never seen a brochure on the trail," Rimmer said. "But I've come this way more than a few times, and I can attest for certain the Raft River is half a day's ride ahead of us. I can attest for certain, too, that it's a point of interest."

Rimmer laughed at his own joke.

"Yes, sir. It's a point of interest all right. Damn near ever time I've come through this way, that Raft River is flooded. We'll have no choice but to float the wagons and swim the animals. We'll be a day just getting from one side to the other. But it ain't swift like the Snake, so there's small chance of anyone drowning. But anything can happen when you start throwing wagons and oxen and horses and women and children into a body of water. Yep. They should write it up in that brochure, because the Raft River is a definite point of interest."

"And we'll come to it tomorrow?" Marie asked.

Rimmer looked at the rock formations around them and gave his beard a scratch.

"These rocks here, I remember them well. It seems to me they're a half day's ride from the Raft River. But with the wagons and the rate we're going, maybe it's a day and a half. I'd hope that tonight we would camp near the river and cross it tomorrow. If we don't reach the river by tonight, we'll have to make a decision when we do reach it because it's a full day's job to get from one side to t'other."

"It is one hardship after another, Mr. Rimmer," Marie said.

"It is, ma'am. I reckon that's why so many don't bother coming out here. Suits me fine, though. The harder the journey, the more people don't come. Keeps this country from getting overrun with folks. If they was a good road from New York City to Oregon City, with ferries and bridges and all the rocks cleared away? Well, hell, we'd have nothing but people out here."

"I suppose that's true," Marie said. "Are people so bad?"

Rimmer chuckled.

"For a man like me? Yes, ma'am. Fewer the better. Well, I better move on to the front of the wagons and ask your brother if his brochure has any advice on getting across the Raft River. Maybe some man settin' back east writing up brochures has some ideas I ain't thought of yet."

Rimmer laughed again and shook his head and gave his reins and tug and started toward the front of the wagon train.

"What does he mean by that?" Marie asked. "A man like him?"

Zeke grinned at her.

"He means a man that don't like to bathe more than once a month."

Marie put her hand up to her face as she laughed some, her eyes glowing brilliantly at her husband. Her fingers slipped up to pinch her nose.

"He does seem to detest soap, doesn't he?"

Zeke grinned at her and nodded his head. But then his face fell serious.

"I think what he means when he says that is that he's not a man who cares to be governed."

Marie nodded her head.

"You're a man who doesn't like to be governed," she said.

Zeke nodded.

"That's true, to a point. But I like to think I can govern myself. I can conduct myself in a civil and decent way."

"And Mr. Rimmer?" Marie said.

"I don't think that man cares to be governed at all. I don't think he wants to be governed by other men or polite society or acceptable norms or even by his own self."

"You don't like him?" Marie asked, her voice just a whisper now.

"It's not that I dislike him. If he does the job we're paying him to do, I've got nothing to hold against him. But I think he's a dangerous man, and untrustworthy. If we'd not been delayed to Bridger's Fort, and I'd have had the opportunity to give input on the matter, I would have urged Elias not to hire him."

"Elias is a good judge of character."

"He is," Zeke agreed. "But he's also feeling the pressure of all these lives depending on his good judgment. And I think he hired Rimmer and those others because they were all that was available. Personally, I'd rather trust that brochure writer back east."

Marie watched her husband's face become rigid with concern as he looked down the row of wagons at Rimmer still riding up toward the lead wagon.

"He and his men have been helpful," Marie said. "They did hard work in getting the wagons down that mountain spur."

"They did work hard," Zeke agreed. "And if there's anything Elias can do, it's spot a man who is capable of putting his back into a job."

Zeke took a breath and then offered his wife a smile.

"We'll be all right. I'm probably thinking too much about it. They've gotten us this far without incident."

"Except for the Barnes girl," Marie pointed out.

Zeke nodded.

"Well, that's true. And if hadn't been for the theft back at the fort, that man Norwood would have been part of our company."

MIDMORNING THE NEXT DAY, Elias rode Tuckee up to the top of a hill. The wagon train still below him wound its way through a zigzag maze of low hills, looking like a snake slithering along.

Neil Rimmer had told him of the Raft River and Elias consulted his brochure to find nothing about crossing the river. The only mention of the river in the brochure was that this was the "parting of the ways." Those bound for California would follow the Raft River to the south. It would take them south to the famed City of Rocks and from there they would follow a series of creeks to the Humboldt River. Elias's brochure told him that much, but made no mention of Oregon Trail emigrants crossing the Raft River.

"Well, I can tell you for sure you'll have to cross it," Rimmer laughed, casting aspersions on eastern writers. "Beaver dams usually back this river up pretty good. If it's as high as it was last time I come through this way, you'll have to float your wagons."

That had been the previous afternoon. They'd broken camp early, rolling out before six o'clock in the morning and come five miles. Rimmer's last word to Elias, just a half hour ago, had been a prediction that they'd be upon the Raft River soon.

Looking over his shoulder from the top of the hill where he now sat, Elias had just a glimpse of the Snake River. They were about a mile south of the river. Its banks now were steep on the both sides, and a man had to be at just the right height with the interceding hills sitting just low enough, to see the river. He took a heavy breath and craned his neck. Now, up ahead, he saw something that caught him by surprise. The familiar plumed shape of two dozen covered wagons, just parked on a hill about two miles on.

"There's a wagon train up ahead!" Elias called down to no one in particular.

A couple of the men riding horses veered from the trail to join Elias at the top of the hill to see for themselves. Everyone welcomed any alteration from the mundane that did not increase the hardship.

Wiser McKinney was among those who mounted the hill.

"That'll be Mr. Hedden's wagon train," Wiser said. "That man who tried to drown me as a thief."

"Probably so," Elias said. "I'm not sure why they're stopped, but it'll give you another chance to thank him for not finishing the job."

Wiser shook his head, a look of disgust flashing across his face.

"Truth be told, I'd rather not see the man again."

The wagons kept snaking through the maze of hills down below, but several of the men just sat their horses there on the hill, watching the stationary wagons up ahead. A few young boys came running up the hill, laughing and chasing each other, and they peppered "Mr. Elias" with questions about the distant wagons.

After a while of this, Elias clicked his tongue and gave Tuckee a touch on the shoulder with his heel, and the horse nodded his head and started forward. Elias rode out past the other pioneers to the front of the wagon train and then left it behind, covering the distance to the wagons he'd seen out ahead of him.

This company of emigrants was still camped, but something about the scene didn't make sense. Their livestock grazed down in a low valley, but they also had their wagons parked down there. The wagons Elias had seen from the distance were still another forty yards or so farther than the main part of this company. Those wagons were parked up on a high hill.

A fair number of the emigrants as Elias rode near their camp looked to be shoring up their wagons – applying axle grease, stitching canvas, adjusting their loads. Some of them were hauling firewood back to their wagons from a lines of trees farther along. Elias also realized that this was not Hedden's wagon train, but another that had left out of Fort Bridger a day or two ahead of the Townes Party. These folks were bound for California.

One of them, a man named Cooper, Elias had met back at Bridger's Fort.

"Morning, Mr. Townes," Cooper said, walking out toward Elias.

"Mr. Cooper! I didn't expect to see you again in this lifetime," Elias said.

"We were delayed back at Fort Hall," Cooper said. "We spent some extra days doing some hunting and smoking meat up near the fort."

"And you're camped here for the day?"

"Got here a couple of days ago. We're preparing to make the big push south beginning tomorrow."

"So this will be it," Elias said. "You go south and we keep moving west."

"A man can never say for certain where his life might take him, but I suspect this will be our last parting," Cooper said. And then he gave a chuckle. "I think once you get past this next rough patch, you won't want to come back."

"Next rough patch?" Elias said.

"You haven't seen it yet," Cooper said. "You've got a crossing to make over that hill."

Cooper pointed to the hill ahead, where Elias had seen the wagons. He looked at them now and, this close, realized the canvas on the wagons was tattered and there was an array of abandoned items scattered around the wagons. He could see stoves and furniture, what looked like bed frames and dressers and chairs.

"Is this yours?" Elias asked.

Cooper shook his head.

"Abandoned. My best guess is that people heading west saw that river over the bluff and decided to leave their wagons and pack from here."

"Is it so bad?" Elias said.

"Wide, and deep. It'll be troublesome to get across it."

Elias glanced back. His own wagons were not yet caught up, but some of the saddled men were now nearing them.

"I suppose I'd better go and have a look," Elias said.

Cooper nodded.

"If we don't speak again, I wish good luck to you, Mr. Townes."

"And the same to you, Mr. Cooper."

Tuckee had spent the morning at a walk, and as soon as Elias turned him to the hill he broke into a trot and took the hill in a few bounds. As they neared the top, Elias had to bring him around the abandoned possessions. Some of it was nice furniture, pieces that must have been hard to part with. And when he reached the top of the hill, Elias saw why people had abandoned their things.

The Raft River looked more like an enormous lake. Hundreds of yards wide, at a glance Elias could see that they would have to float their wagons. He shook his head in dismay.

"It's not too late to come to California with us!" Cooper shouted from down below, and Elias couldn't help but grin at the man.

"It's a tempting offer!" Elias called back.

THEY WASTED NO TIME.

Elias found Rimmer who sent for his men who were back behind the wagon train with the cow column. Rimmer and his men determined the best spot for crossing the river.

"It's the beaver dams," Rimmer complained. "They've got this whole thing blocked up. I bet not more than a trickle of this river even gets into the Snake River. The good things is, the water ain't moving. That'll make the crossing easier to manage."

"Maybe we should just settle here and become trappers," Elias suggested.

Rimmer laughed and shook his head.

"I'd recommend it if there was any money to be made in furs anymore."

Rimmer led the Townes party to the south, avoiding the bluff where the abandoned supplies and wagons prevented passage. They'd found a relatively narrow spot in the flooded valley where dry land on one bank was separated from dry land on the other bank by only about a hundred and fifty feet. It was a gentle but tall rise on the west bank that would give them a spot to beach the wagons.

And now came the tedious work.

Emigrants applied axle grease to the wagons wherever they saw a crack or space between board that would let water through. They dropped down their canvas coverings and removed the bows. Every family worked at the same time to prepare the wagons.

"You must be sure of your loads," Elias cautioned as he moved up and down the wagon train, helping people or watching to be sure they were doing all they could in preparation for the crossing. "Any uneven weight could turn your wagon over in the middle of this river. If a wagon goes over, it will be lost, and all the supplies inside it."

It was here that some families finally opted to toss heirloom pieces of furniture out of their wagons that, up to now, they'd refused to relinquish. A dresser here. A top-heavy stove there. Most everyone seemed now to understand that anything not necessary for immediate survival would have to be abandoned. But there were plenty who had come before and tossed their belongings, and across the river on the far bank, someone spotted and pointed out to the others the remnants of what could happen to those who still refused to give up anything that wasn't a necessity. There on the bank, an overturned wagon bed was broken apart and rotting, the remains of some other traveler's stubbornness.

While this work went on, the Tucker brothers and the Page brothers, with Zeke helping, felled three good sized cottonwood trees. Using every branch of decent size and the trunks, they quickly built two rafts that could float the undercarriages from the wagons. The rafts would have to go back and forth across the flooded plain, and that meant lengths of rope had to be tied together.

No one shirked.

If Elias or Henry Blair or Rimmer or anyone else saw someone standing still for more than a moment, a job for that man could quickly be found.

And then it was time to begin the crossing.

George Long and the other packers swam their horses and mules across. Their supplies would come over on the rafts. The lack of swift current made swimming the livestock over not a terribly difficult job, though convincing some of the mules and horses to go into the water required a great deal of thrashing and splashing and shouting. Eventually, though, all six men with their animals were across. Long toted with him one end of a rope tied to one of the rafts. Another man carried the rope tied to the other raft.

Elias paid no attention to the time.

He'd given up any thought of ever reaching Oregon City. Now, his only purpose in life was to get to the other side of this river. He couldn't think about tomorrow. He couldn't think about the many more miles in front of him. And he knew every man in the company was the same way. Any thought of how many more rivers they would have to cross like this, and they'd all turn around and go back.

A crew of the hardest working men staged at the river bank. There, one by one, they removed the undercarriage from the wagons. There was no other way to do it. They used heavy poles and strong backs to slide down the loaded wagon beds. And then they muscled those wagon beds into the water.

The first wagon to go across belonged to Walter Brown.

Brown's wife and daughters crowded into the wagon, all of them staying as near to the center as they could. Brown and two of Rimmer's men launched the wagon into the water. One of the girls let out a scream as the wagon tipped precariously. Then Brown and one of Rimmer's men got into the wagon with poles one fore and one aft, and they began pushing the wagon across the swollen river.

A tree branch or a hidden rock just under the surface would easily have sent the whole pack of them into the water, and the women and children watching from the bank held their breath.

"Oh! How it tips!" Marie said to Madeline, and she held Daniel tight against her.

As Brown's wagon moved out across the river, the men on the far bank began pulling the raft with Brown's undercarriage across. A couple of men on the eastern bank held their rope to keep it taut so the raft didn't drift away.

As Brown's wagon got about forty yards out into the water, Captain Walker's wagon was ready to go, and the men at the bank launched the next wagon.

Elias stood near the bank and watched. Ready to dive in and try to make a rescue if he had to.

They kept the wagons moving like this. Two or three on the river at any given moment. The rafts going back and forth.

Had there been more trees along the banks, they might have employed the rafts to ferry the wagons across, but the supply of trees was so limited – and the good ones nearly all already chopped down – that they didn't have rafts big enough or sturdy enough to float the wagons.

As the wagons continued to go and the numbers on the eastern bank dwindled, some of the men who made it to the far bank rode back on the rafts to help get the last of the wagons across.

After the first few families crossed in their wagons, Elias decided it was safer to put women and children on the rafts and let the men pole the wagons across.

With each crossing of the rafts, Elias urged mothers to keep a hold on their young children.

"Sit in the middle of the raft," Elias would say to them. "No! Do not stand, and don't dangle your feet over the side."

A catastrophe could not only mean the loss of life, but it would mean the loss of time. And time now weighed as heavily on Elias as anything. Rimmer's constant warnings of snow had convinced him – delay might mean disaster for them all.

By the time Zeke pushed his wagon into the river, and he and Caleb Driscoll started to pole the wagon across, the far bank was all but clear of wagons.

Elias had gone just in front of him, and the men on the far bank were just now getting the wagon bed up onto the undercarriage.

Not a man, woman, or child in the party was dry. Some had swam with animals. Two had fallen out of their wagons during the crossing, but fortunately the worst of it was they'd gotten wet. Some had crossed back and forth on the hastily made rafts where the water freely seeped up between the logs. But even those who managed to never get a drop of river water on them were drenched in sweat – their shirts and pants soaked through.

At dusk, the men in the cow column stripped down to their undergarments. Then they whooped and hollered and waved their hats and shouted and drove the livestock down into the water to swim across.

Zeke thought it a small miracle, but they didn't lose a steer or a cow. No horse, none of the oxen, none of the goats. No animals were lost in the crossing.

"Water ain't moving," Rimmer remarked upon hearing Zeke declare it a miracle. "If the water was moving – like the Snake up yonder – it would be easier to count the cattle we have left than count the ones we lost."

THE TOWNES PARTY CAMPED that night just beyond the Raft River. For the whole day, they'd managed less than ten miles.

At dawn, the exhausted emigrants were just rising from their beds. The morning was cold and many of the men complained of being sore from the previous day's labor. Fires were slow to get lit. Breakfasts slow to cook. Clothes that hung through the night on strings tied between wagons were still damp and cold.

Elias knew in the mornings he could count on the women. If their husbands and sons were exhausted from a day's work but Elias was eager to get moving, the women would roust out the men. The women who wanted off the trail in the worst way. The women who simply wanted to be in their new place, building their new homes, getting accustomed to their new lives. They were the ones who could keep this wagon train moving better than any drover.

But this morning, even the women moved slow.

"I'm worried about Reverend Marsh and his wife when they get to this river," Elias confided in Rimmer.

"Henry Temple can get them across it," Rimmer said. "One wagon ain't as hard as all of these. Two good men can get it done. I've seen Henry get a canoe down the Missouri that was piled ten feet high with pelts. And we left a raft on the bank for them, with poles. They'll be able to get across easier than we did."

Elias nodded his head.

"I have to trust you," he said. "You know the man, and I don't. But that was a helluva battle getting over that river yesterday. I hate the thought of them trying to do it with just the four of them. I wonder if we should wait today and move tomorrow."

"You can't afford to lose another day, Mr. Townes," Rimmer said. "There's plenty more crossings to make, and none of them easier than yesterday's. You've seen the way the currents move on the Snake River, and we have to cross that at least twice."

Still, it was mid-morning before the Townes Party started moving away from the Raft River, continuing on with the Snake River off their right shoulders.

11

"YOU FEELING BETTER?" HENRY Temple asked, reaching for the tin pot on the rock beside the fire.

Reverend Marsh rubbed his eyes against the morning sun.

"I was in a bad way, Mr. Temple," Marsh said. "But I do feel somewhat restored this morning."

Temple grabbed the handle on the pot and then jerked his hand back. He laughed a bit.

"That there is a mite hot," he laughed.

Among Rimmer's men, Henry Temple was the oldest by far. Though Rimmer had said it as a joke, Temple had come out west with the Hudson Bay Company nearly twenty years before. He'd been a young man then, and at the time there was nothing out here but a few rough timber structures, Indians, and bear. And beaver. Beaver by the tens of thousands. A man couldn't cross a stream without stepping on two of them back in those days. And the Hudson Bay Company men had trapped every one they could find.

Temple had come west fleeing a warrant in Philadelphia. He'd abused his wife there, nearly beat her to death in a drunken rage. So he dropped his given name and started calling himself Henry Temple. The Hudson Bay men readily accepted him. Half of them were fleeing warrants.

When the market for beaver pelts fell apart, Temple decided to stay in the west. It wasn't so much that he worried about the warrant. So long as he stayed away from Philadelphia, he didn't figure it would ever be a concern. Not after so many years. Hell, at times he had trouble remembering his given name. He didn't think anyone back east would remember it, either.

Instead, he stayed in the west because a man could live without being bothered here. He could hunt for his supper and live whatever way he wanted. He married a squaw. Left that one after a while and married another. He had little halfbreed babies he hadn't seen in five or ten years and hoped to never see again. He made his living however he could. Hauling freight from Independence, Missouri, to the western forts.

He'd only recently joined up with a man called Hubbard who was running freight to Bridger's Fort. Hubbard and his outfit went on a hunting expedition in the Wind River Mountains. They were hunting Injun scalps, and when they came across a summer village in the Winds where the men were all off hunting game, Hubbard and his outfit took every scalp they could find. Women and children and old folks. One or two of the boys got a stab wound for their troubles, but they all made it out without serious injuries.

Hubbard made off for Missouri, and Henry Temple figured he was about halfway there by now. Maybe even closer. And most of the outfit went with Hubbard.

But Rimmer wasn't interested in going back east, and a small group stayed with him.

Henry Temple didn't like Neil Rimmer any better than he liked Hubbard. But he did like staying out west as opposed to going back to Missouri.

Temple used the tail of his shirt, wrapped it around his hand once, and grabbed the handle of the pot. He poured himself some coffee. Black stuff that would have to be chewed rather than drank.

"Can I pour you a cup, preacher?"

Reverend Marsh blanched at the suggestion and shook his head.

"No, thank you. I fear I need to recover before I indulge."

"Got to keep that strength up," Temple said. "We've got rough miles ahead of us, and we're going to have to move fast to catch back up to them others."

"Indeed," Reverend Marsh said. But when Temple gestured at him with the coffee pot again, Marsh waved it off.

Henry Temple was a large man. Broad shoulders, barrel chest. He had salt-and-pepper hair and beard that all sort of entangled together, giving Reverend Marsh to think of an animal costume for a stage performance. Henry Temple looked more a caricature of a bear or a buffalo than an actual man. He wore a dirty shirt and britches he tied with a length of rope. Moccasin boots that were stained and wearing thin in places. Maybe it was all that hair, or the dirt that seemed to cling to the exposed parts of his face, but he had an angry and mean look to him. Mrs. Marsh did not care for the man and had taken pains to avoid him even while her husband was sick.

Rimmer had left a boy named Hayton with him. Kid couldn't have been more than twenty years old. A greenhorn still wet behind the ears. Rimmer should have knowed better than to leave a kid like that with a man like Henry Temple. Generally speaking, Henry Temple didn't like people. Specifically, he didn't like greenhorns. Hayton was more greenhorn even than the preacher. But Temple's opinion was that Hayton would learn and the preacher wasn't going to make it.

"What are your plans when you get to Oregon City, preacher?"

"I intend to minister to the Natives in that part of the country," Reverend Marsh said.

"You ain't worried about preaching to the savages?" Temple asked. "You'll be lucky to survive more'n a few months before them savages decide they want a preacher's scalp."

"'He who dwells in the shelter of the Most High will abide in the shadow of the Almighty,'" Reverend Marsh said, straightening his shoulders a bit.

"I ain't never had much churchin'," Henry Temple muttered from behind his beard. "What's that mean?"

"It means that I find refuge in my God," Reverend Marsh said. "I am affiliated with the Methodist Church. We have a church there in Oregon City. The pastor is a friend of mine, and it was at his invitation that I undertook –"

But that was as far as Reverend Marsh got in his story.

Henry Temple grabbed the coffee pot again, but this time he grabbed it by the neck, not the handle, and without the benefit of his shirt or anything else to protect his bare hand. He screamed. A guttural, wild scream that sounded more like a grizzly bear than a man. And he flung the near-boiling contents of the kettle directly at Marsh. The lid broke free and fell away. The coffee, or some major portion of it, splashed into the preacher's face.

Reverend Marsh threw up his hands and recoiled, but too late. The scalding coffee blinded him and burned his skin. He let out a terrified yelp, but Henry Temple's meaty fist crashed into the side of Reverend Marsh's head.

Temple dashed forward, bowling the man over, and landed on top of him. His long knife was out, and he plunged it now, several times into the preacher's chest. Reverend Marsh threw up his hands to try to protect himself, but he was too weak to offer any sort of defense.

Again and again Temple rose up and then crashed down, thrusting the knife into the preacher's chest and neck. Blood splattered. A dozen or more times, and the preacher had stopped moving. A sickening sound of death emitted from his mouth as he gasped for air.

LILLIAN MARSH SCREAMED.

She'd been on the other side of the wagon when she heard the commotion and came around to see the big man murdering her husband.

His chest rising and falling in great breaths, Henry Temple looked up a the preacher's wife.

His face reminded her of every imagining she'd ever had of Lucifer. Wild and covered in blood. Dark eyes full of hatred. A snarl at the lips. Her first instinct was to go to her husband, but this madman straddled over him and looked his blood lust upon her.

Lillian Marsh did not know what to do other than to turn and run. But she stumbled straightaway and had to regain herself. She knew, without even looking back, that Temple pursued her. Her ankle turned on a loose rock and this time she spilled onto the ground.

Temple pounded.

He drove his knife through her tiny frame with such force that it pinned her to the ground. But she did not make a sound, even as Temple wrenched and twisted and pulled the knife, lifting her slightly off the ground before it jerked free.

Now she whimpered.

Temple fell on her, not with the same ferocity with which he attacked her husband, but certainly a sufficient amount. He stabbed her three more times in the back, and then he cut her throat.

Hayton appeared, coming from the grass a ways from the wagon where the livestock grazed. By this time, Henry Temple had gone to the preacher's water barrel and was splashing water on his face and hands to clean himself.

"What did you do?" Hayton asked.

Temple grunted at him and splashed more water on his face.

"Tell me what you did," Hayton said.

"We got to catch up to the others," Temple said. "They're two days in front of us. If we don't get moving, we might never catch them."

"But why did you kill the preacher and his wife?"

"He started talking his Bible talk at me. I don't stand for Bible talk. If I wanted Bible talk, I would have gone on back to Missouri with Hubbard and them."

Hayton took a breath and shook his head.

"I don't understand you," he said. "Rimmer told us to make sure nothing happened to these people. He said he wanted them to catch back up safe and sound so that Townes don't mistrust us."

"Rimmer don't tell me what to do," Temple said. "We need to pack up and get moving."

Hayton shook his head.

"What are we going to say when we catch back up? How are we going to explain that the preacher ain't with us?"

Temple looked at the bodies on the ground, the campsite. He chewed his lip, thinking on it. Then he nodded his head, having reached a conclusion.

"We'll tell them the preacher decided to go back to Fort Hall. We'll say he was still feeling poorly, didn't think he'd be able to start the journey soon enough to catch up. We'll say he insisted that we go on and catch up to the others so we can help the wagon train. We can tell them we argued about it, but the preacher insisted, and so we went on without him and his wife. Last we saw them, they was going on back to Fort Hall. And that's all we know about it," Temple said. He nodded his head again, as if in approval of his lie.

"And what do we do if someone comes by here and finds the preacher. What if it's folks bound for Oregon and they catch up on the trail? They'll know then that we lied."

"They won't know nothing. Anyone who comes across this'll figure Injuns done it. Besides, Rimmer's got it all planned. Ain't nobody going to go the way Rimmer's going to take the Townes Party. Ain't nobody catching up. And soon enough, ain't nobody going to care if the Townes Party knows about what happened here. Now help me search the wagon for any valuables we can take."

Temple made for the wagon to start searching it, but Hayton walked back down toward the livestock.

"Hey! Where are you going?" Temple shouted.

"I'm going to get a couple of oxes so we can hitch them to the wagon and get it turned around. If we're going to say they turned and went back to Fort Hall, we should get them facing toward Fort Hall."

Henry Temple sniffed at the air and then narrowed his eyes, watching Hayton's back as he walked down toward the oxen. His head started bobbing against as he made another decision. His knife was sitting there on the edge of the wagon. He wrapped his fingers around it now and charged at Hayton's back.

12

MOUNTAINS BROKE THE SOUTHERN horizon. The Snake River broke the landscape to the north. Low hills gently rose and fell in front and behind.

But for the most part, the landscape had returned to what they'd grown to know so well – a rolling, grassy prairie with no trees or any other thing to break its distant collision with the sky. Stretching out straight as an arrow over flat land, the trail had returned to its enduring condition, and this was one that was just as dangerous as the steep declines and the water crossings.

The emigrants were again bored.

Gabriel, Elias's older son, rode in the driver's box of the front wagon. He had the lines held loosely in his hand. Sometimes he called out to the oxen. But even they had learned to just keep their heads down and follow the line of tracks already in front of them.

Elias, on his palomino, rode past his son and gave Gabe a nod.

"Everything all right?" Elias said.

"Yes, sir."

"Stay awake, Gabe," Elias said. The boy's eyes looked heavy.

"I'm trying to," Gabe said.

"Boredom leads to carelessness, son. Carelessness leads to accidents."

"Yes, sir."

A few of the mounted men had scattered out over the hills left and right of the trail. Some of the children in the company had run on ahead and were sitting in the grass on a hill out in front of the wagon train. Elias pointed Tuckee to a rise off to the right and when he got to the top, turned the horse back east to watch the wagons passing him.

Zeke and his dogs had dropped far behind the wagons. Zeke sitting there atop the gray, watching the dogs run circles, noses to the ground. They'd found a gopher, Elias decided.

Most of the women and children in the wagon train walked alongside the wagons, staying in the shade cast by the covers. But it was noontime, so the shade was narrow with the sun straight overhead. The men walked out beside the oxen, hats on their heads providing their only shade.

Some men rode horses and hired drivers did the walking. Some of the drivers did their work from the wagons, like Gabe. Especially if they had a box or a seat, though many of the wagons did not have a seat. One or two stood on the braces of the tongue. And wherever they walked or rode or stood, in an hour's time they would be in a different place. Even as he watched, one of the men riding in his wagon climbed down to stand on the tongue's braces and ride there for a while.

Back in Kansas territory, Jeff Pilcher had started counting his steps. He reckoned it took something between two-thousand and twenty-five-hundred steps to make a mile. One night at camp, back in Kansas, they'd gotten a slate and chalk and worked it out. If the trail was two thousand miles and it was two thousand steps to a mile, they'd take more than four million steps on this journey. Of course, none of them would walk the whole thing.

Elias saw Neil Rimmer riding up from the cow column. Rimmer moved quite a bit from the cow column to the front of the wagons and back. His horse came at a trot, and Elias watched as he directed the horse right toward him.

"Mr. Townes," Rimmer said, riding up.

"Pretty day," Townes said, conversationally.

Rimmer shrugged and looked up at the sky, blue as it could be and clear as far as they could see.

"A mite warm," Rimmer said. "But it'll serve."

"What's on your mind, Mr. Rimmer?"

"Well, sir, I'm thinking about the Snake River, Mr. Townes. We've got a couple of choices as to how to get across it, and we'll be at the first of those choices in probably three or four days."

Since clearing the Raft River, they'd made good time. Ten miles one day. A dozen the next. They'd made close to twenty miles the third day out from the Raft River, and if the day kept going as it was, they'd do close to that again today. A twenty-mile day helped considerably to make up for those days when they moved only two or three miles because they encountered a river that had to be forded or the cattle stampeded and they were all afternoon collecting them or some other incident befell them.

"So a decision as to where to cross the Snake River has to be made now?" Elias said.

"Have to be made soon. Yes, sir."

"I have heard of the three islands crossing. Is that the one we're approaching?"

"No, sir. That's the second choice."

Elias held up a hand to delay the conversation. He'd just seen that Zeke left the dogs and was making back toward the wagon train.

"Let's get my brother involved in this discussion," Elias said. He snatched his hat from his head and waved it in the air until he caught Zeke's attention. His younger brother waved back and started to trot Duke in their way.

"I don't mind telling you that I'm impressed with the way this company has moved the last couple of days," Rimmer said. "I wasn't sure you lot had it in you, but we did nigh on twenty miles yesterday, and we're making the same pace today."

Elias nodded.

"None of these folks would be here if they were afraid of walking," Elias laughed.

"I reckon that's true," Rimmer said.

"Speaking of folks who are here and folks who ain't, I wonder when we should expect to see Reverend Marsh and his wife."

Rimmer pursed his lips and gave a small shrug.

"Honestly, Mr. Townes, I would have expected them by now. They've had ample time to catch up to us. All I can figure is that maybe Reverend Marsh took a turn for the worse. If the man's fever persisted and they remained at camp or – God forbid – if he succumbed to his fever." Rimmer finished the sentence with another shrug.

Elias nodded thoughtfully. He'd considered the same possibilities. What worried him was that he wasn't sure he could trust Rimmer and his men, but Temple struck him as one in particular who couldn't be trusted.

"I don't like it any more than you do, Mr. Townes," Rimmer said, reading the look on Elias's face. "But you spend much time here in this part of the country, you learn that you have to accept that sometimes you might never know what happened to someone."

Zeke rode up now close to where Rimmer and Elias sat their horses, and Elias was glad for the opportunity to change the subject.

"Mr. Rimmer says we've got a decision to make," Elias said.

"Crossing the Snake?"

"That's right," Rimmer said. "We're within a few days of the first of two good crossings. We've got the one Mr. Townes mentioned to me just now – the three islands crossing. The other one is the crossing above salmon falls."

"Which is the better crossing?" Zeke asked.

"It's not that one is better than the other," Rimmer said. "The three islands crossing we can probably drive the wagons across. And going from one island to the next, that makes it a little better because we don't have to make the entire length of the river. But, it's deep water for a ford. And if there's been rain upstream, the current could be running pretty fast and we might have to float the wagons. Either way, we're swimming the livestock there."

"What's the other choice?" Zeke said.

"Closer. It puts us on the north side of the Snake River sooner. We'll find good grazing and better water on the north side of the Snake. Like I said, it's upstream of salmon falls. We'd have to float across it, same way we went over Raft River. But the channel at the falls narrows. The water backs up and slows down. The Snake don't run as swift there as it does most everywhere else – including at three islands."

"So the advantage to salmon falls is the water isn't as swift."

"And it puts us on the north side of the river sooner," Rimmer said.

"Which is the easier crossing?" Zeke asked.

Rimmer chuckled.

"Hell, Mr. Townes. Ain't none of 'em easy. And, of course, either way we go, we'll have to cross the Snake again at Fort Boise."

"Fort Boise?" Zeke asked. "I wasn't aware there was another fort before the Blue Mountains."

"It's not much of a fort. Last I was there, it was being run by a French-Canadian called Payette and he had a bunch of Sandwich Islanders working for him. If you thought Fort Hall was light on supplies, this one will be worse. All the folks is friendly, and they keep the nearby Injuns in good spirits with their hospitality. Like as not, we can even hire some local Injuns to ride the livestock across the Snake there. But it ain't a gathering spot the way Bridger's Fort is. You'll not have cause to linger there, outside of just resting. But by the time we get there, the nights will be gettin' a mite chillier, and so you won't want to rest anyhow."

The enormity of the journey still ahead of them began to impress itself upon Elias.

"How far are we to Fort Boise?"

"Well, of course, that depends on where we decide to cross," Rimmer said. "But we're ever bit of two hundred miles still."

"And from Fort Boise on to Oregon City?"

"Another three hundred miles," Rimmer said sourly. "Probably more than that. And that'll be some rough going. It'll require us to negotiate the Blue Mountains, and at the Dalles we'll have to ride the Columbia."

Elias took a heavy breath and frowned at his brother.

"It doesn't feel like we'll ever make it," Elias said.

"Keep your spirits, brother," Zeke said, giving him a grin. "We've come a long way to get downcast now."

"It's August and we've got five hundred miles yet to go. If we don't have another bad day, it'll still be October when we arrive in Oregon City."

"Probably the best thing would be to cross above salmon falls," Rimmer said decisively. "I can't say that one way is any faster than another, but that's probably best. It puts us on the north side of the Snake sooner. Better grass for grazing – and your animals are starting to look like they could use some better grazing. Good water the whole way. It's maybe the tougher crossing, but it would be my advice."

"Then that's the way we should go," Elias said. Zeke nodded agreement. Thinking the discussion was at an end, Zeke started to walk Duke back down toward the wagons, but Rimmer spoke again.

"Of course, we could always go the southern route."

"The southern route?"

Rimmer shrugged and made a face like he wasn't sure he wanted to say anything more.

"It's a trappers' route, is what I'd say," Rimmer said. "None of your emigrants is going that way. That's for sure. But it's a sight easier than either of the crossings of the Snake River. And far less opportunity for loss of life."

"I've never heard anyone mention the southern route," Elias said.

"You wouldn't have," Rimmer said. "Like I told you, it's a trappers' route. You stay south of the Snake River. Don't cross it at all. You follow the Snake River the whole way up. We'll miss Fort Boise, but we ain't missing much. It might be a little more work because you've got to water your livestock in the Snake River, and at times it's tough to find an easy way down the bank to the water. And whatever extra we might add in terms of miles, we more than make up for by not lose two days crossing the river."

"So it's about the same number of miles?"

"About. Sure," Rimmer said.

"Why do other wagon trains not go that route?" Zeke asked.

"The road ain't clear for wagons. But you can see what the countryside looks like as well as I can. It ain't like you're traveling through forests or up and down mountains. It's a little bouncier."

"Trappers are packing," Elias said. "They're leading mules, not wagons."

"True enough," Rimmer conceded.

Elias looked at Zeke, and Zeke shrugged.

"I thought we'd made a decision," Zeke said.

Elias nodded his head.

"I think it's better we go a way that's tried and tested," Elias said. "We'll cross above the falls."

13

NEIL RIMMER HAPPENED TO be riding back with the cow column the next afternoon when he saw a figure appear far behind them on the eastern horizon. A couple of mounted men.

From the distance, Rimmer figured it was probably a couple of Shoshone Injuns, out for a hunt or riding between villages. He paid little attention to the riders. But after some time, he realized that what he was seeing was a single mounted man leading a mule, and Rimmer knew the figure had to be a white man. For one thing, the horse wasn't an Indian pony. For another, the rider was a large man wearing a hat. Not that Indians couldn't set a hat upon their head, but any man who'd spent as long as Rimmer out in these parts knew the difference between a white man on a horse and an Indian on a pony.

"Hey!" Rimmer called to Jerry Bennett. "We've got somebody riding up behind us."

Jerry nearly jerked himself out of the saddle he turned so fast to see.

"Who the hell is that?" Jerry said.

"Well, I don't know, Jerome. Maybe you and me ought to ride toward him some and see."

Jerry rode a sleek bay with a black mane, and he turned his horse now toward Will Page. Like Jerry, Will and his brother Cody planned to work for Elias and Zeke Townes when they arrived in Oregon City. They afforded this trip because the Townes brothers were paying them wages to drive the cattle and had supplied the wagon that carried all their supplies.

"Somebody's back behind us," Jerry told Will, and Will Page just about had the same reaction Jerry'd had. "Me and Rimmer is gonna ride back and see what it's about."

"What do you want me to do?" Will asked.

"Just kind of keep a watch, and if we get attacked by a hundred Injuns coming up out of the low places and out from behind hills, maybe you ought to leave the cattle and go warn the folks at the wagons."

Will shrugged.

"Be careful," he said.

Rimmer was already started back, and Jerry had to get his horse into a short gallop to catch up to him. When he did catch him, Rimmer was muttering under his breath.

"Something wrong?" Jerry asked.

"It's Henry Temple," Rimmer said.

Jerry squinted at the man ahead of them, still too far off for Jerry to make out any identifying features.

"You sure?"

"Of course I'm sure," Rimmer said. "You ride with a man in your outfit and you learn to recognize him. Don't you?"

"I suppose," Jerry said. "But I don't recognize him."

"Well, I do. And if he's coming on our backtrail by hisself, that means something bad has happened."

Rimmer took a heavy breath and glanced at Jerry. For a moment, Jerry wondered if Rimmer was sizing him up, trying to decide something. Jerry glanced back at the cow column to see if Will Page was watching. He was not.

"I like to never catch you up!" Henry Temple shouted from distance.

Rimmer touched his horse with his heel and called to him to speed him up. Jerry held back, kept his horse at a walk to see how this reunion would play out before he joined in with them. Rimmer's behavior since recognizing Temple left Jerry feeling uncomfortable.

Rimmer's horse galloped directly toward Temple, and when the two men reached each other, both reined up. They exchanged words for just a couple of moments. Rimmer seemed agitated. But then he wheeled his horse. Temple gave a rough tug to the mule and started coming toward Jerry at a walk.

Rimmer trotted up to Jerry.

"Would you go and fetch Mr. Townes for me?" Rimmer said.

"Which one?"

"The captain of the wagon train," Rimmer snapped.

Jerry chuckled a little.

"Sure. I'll go and get him. Is there a problem?"

"I'd rather tell Townes myself."

JERRY BENNETT FOUND ELIAS Townes all the way in the lead of the wagon train. Elias was walking beside his wife. Both of them held the leads for their horses, but their saddles were riding on the back of the wagon.

"Mr. Townes," Jerry called as he came near to them.

"Jerry? Everything all right?"

"I couldn't say, Mr. Townes. Mr. Rimmer back there with the livestock, he asked that I ride forward to get you. He wants to have a word."

Elias frowned.

"Do you know what about?"

"Yes, sir. That man Henry Temple? He's come back."

Elias furrowed his brow.

"And Reverend Marsh?"

"No, sir. No sign of Reverend Marsh. And Rimmer seems a mite agitated."

Elias flashed a look of concern at his wife.

"I'd better ride back," he said, and then let out a heavy sigh. "It's always some calamity."

Jerry dropped down from his own saddle to help. He held the horse while Elias walked back and forth to the moving wagon to get first the saddle blanket and then the saddle. He had to jog ahead twenty yards to get the bridle. The wagons only ever seemed to move fast when a man needed them to stand still.

Madeline kept casting worried looks over her shoulder, but she continued to walk, pulling her pony along behind her.

"I had intended to walk the rest of the afternoon," Elias told Jerry Bennett. "I wanted to give Tuckee a rest today. We're going to cross the Snake soon and we need to make sure all our horses are plenty rested. You're rotating horses in the remuda?"

"I am, yes, sir," Jerry said. "Every morning I take a different horse."

"Good. The other boys are, too?"

"They are."

Elias paid little attention to the cow column. These men were well capable of governing themselves. They were men accustomed to hard work who needed little overseeing on a trail. So as he peppered Jerry with questions, really all he was doing was just making conversation while he got Tuckee saddled. Once the palomino was ready, Elias stepped into the stirrup and pulled himself up onto the horse's back. Jerry Bennett had waited for him, and now the two of them rode together back toward the cow column.

Several of the emigrants in the wagon train had steers or milk cows among the livestock, and they cast curious and worried looks at Elias and

Jerry as they rode past. If it was a stampede or if Indians had driven off some of the livestock, the emigrants knew they might have lost valuable livestock. Whatever it was, they all knew that Elias seldom rode back to the cow column unless there was a problem.

As Elias approached the cow column, he could see Rimmer and another man riding together, the other one leading a mule. Elias figured that was Henry Temple, returned without Reverend Marsh and his wife. Now Rimmer broke free, leaving the other man behind, and trotted forward to meet Elias.

"Mr. Townes," Rimmer said. "There's been some trouble."

"So I gather," Elias said. "Tell me about it."

"Henry Temple has just returned. He says the preacher's condition hadn't improved much after a couple of days, and so the boy, Hayton, agreed to take Reverend Marsh and his wife back to Fort Hall. They'll winter there and finish their journey come spring. Truth is, Henry says he don't know that the preacher will make it to winter. Says his fever got worse."

"I'd like to hear it from Mr. Temple," Elias said, and he let Tuckee gallop down toward the cow column and toward Temple. Rimmer followed not far behind him.

"Hey there, Mr. Townes," Temple said. "I guess Rimmer told you."

"I'd like for you to tell me," Elias said.

"Sure. That first day you left us, the preacher seemed to be on the mend. But then his fever took worse. Shakes and shivering and sweating all at the same time. The man was in a poorly state. We waited another day or two, and he didn't improve much. I says to Mrs. Reverend Marsh that we had to go or we'd never catch you. She says the reverend's too sick to move. So I says it's move or stay here for good."

"And Reverend Marsh? His condition got worse?"

"Well, not no better. Maybe not no worse, neither."

"And then what happened?"

"Hayton come up with the solution. That boy's a good 'un. He says, why don't he stay with the preacher and his wife until the preacher is fit to move, and then he'll take 'em on back to Fort Hall. And he says I should move on, catch up to the wagon train, so that you know what become of the preacher."

"And that was amenable to Mrs. Marsh?" Elias asked.

"I don't know what you mean by that."

"He's asking if Mrs. Marsh agreed to that," Rimmer cut in.

"Oh, she agreed. She said Fort Hall for the winter would be fine. So I come back, and I guess by now they're back to Fort Hall."

More than anything, Elias wanted to send someone back to check on Reverend Marsh. He wanted to hear the story from Reverend Marsh. Would they tell it different? Had Temple for some reason bullied them into returning to Fort Hall? Did something else happen? Elias thought of what Marsh had told him back at Bridger's Fort. He carried donations for not only his own ministry but also for a mission at Walla Walla. Reverend Marsh hadn't confided exactly how much money he carried, but he led Elias to believe the sum was significant. Could Temple have found that money?

Rimmer saw the consternation on Elias's face, but he misread it. Maybe.

"Don't you worry about them, none," Rimmer said. "Hayton's young, but he's a good boy and he's got good sense. He'll get the preacher back to Fort Hall, no problem."

Elias gave a tug to Tuckee's reins and started back toward the wagon train. He'd have to let the others know that Reverend Marsh wouldn't be joining them.

On the ride back toward the wagons, Elias caught himself hanging his head. Everything somehow seemed worse.

"YOU KILLED THAT PREACHER, didn't you?" Rimmer said. "I covered for you with Townes, but I know that business about them going back to Fort Hall is a lie."

It was night. Rimmer and Temple were riding watch on the livestock, though they weren't doing that. They'd ridden out some ways away from the rest of the hands camping with the livestock. And now they were talking where they wouldn't be overheard.

"They went back to Fort Hall, just like I told you. The preacher wasn't feeling no better. Hayton volunteered to take them back to Fort Hall."

Temple stuck to his lie. It was easier to do in the dark where a man couldn't read a face or the eyes. But Rimmer didn't need to see his face or his eyes. Rimmer knew the man, or knew enough men just like him.

"Tell me the truth," Rimmer said. "What did you do to the preacher?"

"What if I did kill him?" Temple said.

"The woman, too?"

"What if I did?"

"What happened to Hayton?" Rimmer asked.

"What if I killed him, too?"

Rimmer shook his head.

"Why would you do that? Didn't I tell you before we left you with the preacher, be sure you get them caught up to the wagon train safe and sound? Didn't I say that to you?"

Temple mumbled a bit. Tried to dissemble some. But then finally he fessed up to the whole thing.

"You're the reason I done it," Temple said. "You should've never said to me that I had to get them back. I started thinking on that, you telling me what to do like that. And I started getting angry about it. And that preacher, talking all his God talk at me. Quoting the Bible at me. So I killed him, and then I killed the woman."

"And Hayton?"

"I didn't trust him," Temple said after a moment. "He started walking off after he saw them two dead. I didn't know where he was going."

Rimmer chuckled.

"Where the hell would he be going? You're out in the middle of nowhere."

"Well, he was walking off, and I didn't know what he had in mind. So I put him down, too."

Rimmer was silent for a long time. When he finally did speak, his voice was strained, and Temple knew the man was furious but trying to hold back his temper.

"We've got something cooking here," Rimmer said. "We lucked into a whole wagon train of greenhorns who don't know nothing about nothing. We can do with them whatever we want. If we want to force them to pay more, we can do it. If we want to separate them, and kill them all, we can do it. We can make it look like Injuns done it. No problem. If we want to steal from them the whole way down the trail, we can do that. But if you foul this up so they don't trust me, we can't do nothing."

"I ain't trying to foul nothing up," Temple cut in.

"Listen to me. I'm planning to take them the southern route."

"The southern route?" Temple said. "There ain't no southern route."

Rimmer chuckled.

"I know that. And you know that. But them greenhorns don't know that.

"Are you talking about the trapper's trail south of the Snake? That ain't fit for wagons."

"That's exactly what I'm talking about. We're gonna keep to the south of the Snake River. I'm going to talk them into it so good, they're going to think it was their idea. And when we're out there, out where we won't see no other wagons nor forts nor nothing else, that's when we can do what we want. We can take their women. We can cut their throats. We can steal all their livestock. Whatever we want to do because they will be at our mercy. Completely."

"Yeah," Temple said. "I get it."

"Yeah? So you understand? You understand I've got a plan here?"

"Sure. I get it."

"Then why are you trying to foul it up?" Rimmer hissed. "I've been working all this time to get Townes to trust me. But now he ain't sure again. He thinks you're lying about the preacher, and he's wondering if I'm as untrustworthy as you are. Now I've got to convince him that your lie is true and he can still trust me."

"I don't like you talking to me like this," Temple snarled. "I ain't no child for you to discipline."

"I got plans," Rimmer said. "Big plans. And I need you to cooperate with me so we can make those plans happen. We're already down two men now. It's just five of us left. It makes it harder if it's just five of us."

"Who shot Norwood?" Temple said. "That was you."

"He should've never killed that girl," Rimmer said, his voice dropping a touch.

Temple guffawed. Loud, sounding even louder through the silence of the night.

"Hush!" Rimmer snapped. "You want to wake the whole camp?"

"I know what happened to that girl," Temple said. "Don't you put that off on Norwood. I seen you. I seen you watching her and the boy, and I seen you sneak around that hill. I know who snatched her and took her down into that canyon."

The silence returned now to the night. Not even the harsh, whispered argument of before. The two men deathly silent.

And then, after more than a minute had passed without a word between them, Rimmer spoke.

"How much did you take off that preacher?"

Temple chuckled.

"A goodly sum," he said. "Almost three hundred dollars."

"You keep it," Rimmer said.

Temple chuckled again.

"I intend to," he said.

"I mean, I ain't gonna tell you to split it with me and the boys. That's all yours. But I need you to cooperate with me, now. This can be a big haul for us. If that preacher had three hundred, who knows how much the rest of them might have."

"We're just five men, like you said," Temple said. "How are we supposed to deal with an entire wagon train?"

"One at a time. And we separate them. And we make them quarrel with each other."

"If you're planning to take them on the southern route, how come we're going for the crossing at Salmon Falls?"

"Like I said. I'm planning to make them think it was their idea to go on the southern route. Trust me."

14

ON THE THIRD DAY after Henry Temple's return, Rimmer recommended a halt to the day midway through the afternoon.

"We could keep going," Elias said. "It's still early."

Rimmer had ridden out ahead of the wagon train some distance, and now he shook his head.

"We've got a crossing about three or four miles ahead of us," Rimmer said. "It's Rock Creek we've got to get across. The water isn't the problem. We can ford the creek. But the creek sits in a deep gulch. We'll be most of a day just trying to get down, across, and back out of that gulch. No sense in starting that today. We'll get clear of it tomorrow and still probably make another couple of miles before we lose daylight."

Elias sighed and nodded his head. The short days, where they might have done fifteen miles instead of eight except for some obstacle, these days were infuriating.

"All right, then. We'll stop here if that's what you think is best," Elias said.

They were on a sandy, rocky plain, only fair grass for the livestock. Not an ideal place to camp.

"Let these pilgrims get their camps set, and then anyone who doesn't mind walking a few miles to see a great curiosity should come with us," Rimmer said.

"Come with us where?"

"I've got a curiosity you'll want to see," Rimmer said. "It's two or three miles back, but it's worth the walk. The trail don't go nowhere near it. I bet only the old Hudson Bay men – and the Injuns – even know about it. But what a shame to come all this way, be so close, and not see it. Especially if you don't ever come back this way again."

Elias narrowed his eyes.

"Is it so good?"

"You won't be disappointed," Rimmer grinned.

With much shouting and even some jerking on harnesses or pushing against shoulders, the drivers turned the wagons into a circle. The oxen were turned loose. Young boys and grown men washed the oxen down with water. Some guides would tell emigrants to grease their oxen, at least every few days, but Henry Blair insisted washing them down with water was the right way to do it. Grease would allow dirt and rocks to stick to the hide there under the yoke, and the animals could be rubbed raw on the shoulders. Days could be lost with the teams unable to be harnessed. So the Townes Party used water and brushes on the oxen at the end of each day.

They turned out the horses and the steers and oxen and cows into a flat area where they could found sufficient grass for the livestock to graze. Rimmer's men stayed with the livestock. They didn't have much to do, other than watch for thieving Indians and predators, because not even the horses were bound to wander. After traveling more than a thousand miles, the animals didn't stray too far.

Word spread through the camp that Rimmer had a sight to show off, and several men decided they would join Elias. So when the camp was made, those who were going – making up a body of about a score of mounted men – rode back east. Rimmer kept close to the Snake River canyon. Ever since departing Fort Hall, those who paid attention realized that the Snake River had buried itself deeper and deeper into a canyon. Now, when they caught glimpses of it, the river flowed typically below sight, deep in a canyon sided by vertical escarpments that looked like the ancient ramparts of some medieval castle.

Several of the men at various times rode near enough to look down into the gorge. The water's roar in the deep canyon echoing off the canyons palisades.

Rimmer himself checked several times, eager to be sure he did not miss the sight he wanted to show them.

Elias guessed the gorge had to be five or six hundred yards wide.

Up ahead of where they were, the far side of the canyon jutted in dramatically as the canyon made a wide bend, and here, those near the rim could hear a shift in the quality of the river's roar. It became deeper, stronger.

Rimmer looked back at the others with delighted anticipation.

"It's thunderous," Zeke said.

"It is that!" Rimmer said. "We're close now."

With the water flowing toward them, the small expedition riding back upstream, the first sight they came to was an impressive squeeze of the river as it narrowed to flow between four or five giant rocks that stood vertically like pillars. In a raging white foam, the water gushed between the rocks.

Jeff Pilcher declared it impressive, but not worth the ride back.

Zeke wondered that the water rushing between the pillars could be the cause of the mighty roar emanating from the river canyon.

"Oh, this ain't all I've got to show you," Rimmer said. "It ain't far, now."

They moved along the rim, picking their way through tall grass and sage. Except for a brief jaunt near the edge to look over at the water below, they rode back at a safe distance.

"Mr. Rimmer, how deep do you figure that canyon is?" Elias asked.

Rimmer gave it a glance and then moved his horse closer for a proper look. He turned back toward the other men, a thoughtful look on his face.

"I would bet it's nothing less than four hundred feet from rim to river. Maybe five hundred," Rimmer said. He was still over closer to the edge than anyone else, and then his face lit up. "There it is, gentlemen. Come and have a look!"

Moving over to where Rimmer now sat his horse, the others could just see it now past where the opposite bank jutted forward. Still probably about a mile off, a magnificent drop, falling probably two hundred feet. An inconceivable amount of water dropping over the side every second.

"Oh, my," Zeke breathed. "It's incredible."

"Up here a ways, there's a trail that leads down below the rim where we can get a better look," Rimmer said. "Trappers who've come this way know it's here. And the Injuns gather here sometimes. But you're among the few Anglo men to ever see it. The trail comes right past it. Almost ever emigrant in Oregon has been within five miles of this place and never known it. They go right on by to Rock Creek. Fremont was this way a few years back, and he never saw it, neither. I had a brother in Fremont's company. We met at Bridger's Fort when he was returning, and I asked him about the falls. No idea what I was talking about."

They rode on, most of the men with their eyes fixed on the falls.

Rock buttes rose up over the canyon rims beyond the falls.

The river dropped down a series of ledges, tumbling white and foamy in dozens of streams broken by the enormous protruding rocks. And then it gushed over the big ledge in three wide veils and a dozen smaller ones, tumbling and rolling two hundred feet down into the pool below. The riders could feel the spray blowing cool against their faces.

As much power as any man in the company had ever seen, glorious and awesome in its pure energy, and yet somehow soft and beautiful.

The roar was deafening, especially as they got nearer the falls, and they had to shout to be heard by the man standing next to them.

The sun caught the spray, casting a vivid rainbow through the canyon.

Rimmer led the others down a worn switchback path that hugged the side of the cliff. It dropped down to a wide ledge, sixty feet wide and generally flat. Here the men dismounted and walked to the edge. Down in the canyon below, they could see dozens of Shoshone men and boys fishing with spears. The fishing was successful. Even from the height a couple hundred feet above the Indians, they could see large salmon and trout glistening on the rocks. There were campfires going where fish were cooking. Some of the Shoshone saw the pioneers watching them. A few waved and held up fish to show them.

"The salmon and trout are thick down there below the falls," Rimmer said. "They can't swim farther up the river, so you can reach your hand in the water and bring out as many as you want. I've never come through here when there wasn't dozens of Injuns fishing the banks. Now that they know we're here, they'll come tomorrow and try to sell us baskets of fish."

The men of the Townes Party who made the trip back to the falls reveled in the moment. They relaxed on the rocks, finding shade where they could. The spray of the water falls fell on them and cooled them. Zeke plucked his hat from his head and took off his shirt. He stretched out his arms, letting the tiny drops of water cover him.

Rimmer grinned at Elias.

"Just about makes the last thousand miles worth the ride here, don't it?" he asked.

Elias had to admit that it did.

The next day, as the men worked to get the wagons down into the Rock Creek Canyon and up the other side, the women and children, accompanied by the few men who could be spared, walked back to the falls. Rimmer guided them so that they could all see for themselves. The women took picnics with them, and like their husbands, sat where the spray would cool them in what shade they could find below the escarpments.

15

FROM THE MAGNIFICENT FALLS to the river crossing at the place Rimmer referred to as "salmon falls" was something close to forty miles. Including the day they spent crossing the Rock Creek canyon, it took the Townes Party five days to make it the forty miles. One day lost in the crossing of Rock Creek canyon, and half of another day lost when a storm blew up and dumped rain on them. Buckets and buckets of rain.

What worried Elias was the dark clouds to the north the first two days, and then the third day the rain that drenched the emigrants. The rain lasted the better part of an afternoon, and it came down in wind-driven sheets. A violent downpour. Lightning and thunder. Some of the cattle stampeded in the storm and had to be rounded up, costing the Townes Party another lost day.

But the lost time worried Elias less than the rain. If they were down on the Ohio, Elias knew what that rain would do to the river. It would bring the water level up, the river would run faster. There might be fresh deadfall that would make the water more treacherous. He didn't know the Snake River, but he didn't have any reason to think the Snake would be any different.

Elias got his first look at the crossing in the middle of the afternoon on the fourth day when he and Rimmer and Zeke rode ahead of he wagon train.

"The water is moving fast," Zeke said.

"I never said it moves slow," Rimmer chuckled. "And the rain that's come through the last couple of days, it's filled the river."

"Just makes me wonder if this is the safest place to make our crossing," Zeke said with a sigh.

"There ain't a safe place. But this is the best place, in my opinion. For one thing, this is one of the few places where the river ain't so deep in a canyon. We can actually get down to it. More than anything, that's what makes this an ideal spot."

Zeke looked back over his shoulder. The river canyon was just an easy grade down a short hill. Where the river touched the bank, they'd be able to easily slide a wagon bed down into the water, and get it out again on the other side. Just a mile or two back, the river sat at the bottom of fifty foot vertical basalt cliffs. No way down, not with wagons, anyway. The lay of the land made this an unquestionably good crossing. But the water curled on the surface. Zeke could feel how fast it moved. He could feel that current and how it would grab a man or a wagon bed and all the weight of that deep water would push against him.

"You say there's falls downstream?" Zeke said.

"Nothing like those falls we went to back yonder," Rimmer said. "Just little drops. Six and eight foot drops, maybe. But a serious of them. Maybe a mile downriver, the canyon narrows, pushes all the water down over a series of big shoals."

"What happens if a person or a wagon bed gets caught in that?" Elias asked.

"Nothing good," Rimmer chuckled.

Elias shot a glance at Zeke.

"Because the channel narrows down yonder, the river's kind of backed up into a pool here. It's not as fast as it is in other places. And we've got plenty of river length to float a wagon across before we get swept down to the falls. My advice, Mr. Townes, is to make your crossing here. Get on over to the north side of the Snake River. Good grass on the north side. Good water on the north side. Hell, even from here I can see the tracks of the trail going up the other side over there. There ain't no question that plenty of folks have crossed here in front of us."

Elias nodded his head.

"I see the tracks."

"This is the best way to go," Rimmer said again. "I say bring the wagons up to that bluff yonder and camp there tonight. In the morning, let's start the crossing. It'll take us all day to get across. But on the north side of the Snake River, we can probably move faster. There'll be good grazing for the livestock, so they'll be stronger and better able to lug these wagons every day."

"I hate the thought of crossing this river when it's moving so fast," Elias said.

"We don't have to cross here," Rimmer said. "There's the three island crossing. It's another forty miles or so. But I don't know that it'll be any better than this one, and if we get there and find out it's not, then we'll lose days coming back here."

"We'll make the crossing here," Elias said. "Zeke, why don't you ride ahead and have a look at those falls downstream. I at least want to know what we're dealing with downstream if we lose a wagon. Mr. Rimmer and I will go back to the wagons and bring them here."

AT CAMP THAT NIGHT, with the crossing weighing heavily on everyone's mind, Beth Gordon got to talking to some of the other women.

"Does it make sense to you that Reverend Marsh and his wife would have simply turned back?"

During the journey up the Bear River valley, Lillian Marsh had been a gift to Beth, helping her watch her children. Lillian often carried the Gordon's one-year old son in the wagon as the party moved, or she walked with the young couple's eight-year-old boy, keeping him entertained. And Reverend Marsh had been a frequent encourager to Beth, who in truth had long since lost faith in this journey.

John Gordon and his wife Elizabeth had joined the Townes Party at Bridger's Fort. They had the two sons who kept Beth busy, but she still found time to engage in any bit of gossip that might be moving through the wagon train. John, for his part, kept quiet most of the time and was an eager volunteer when a job needed to be done. But he also never cautioned his wife against gossiping.

"They were very eager to reach the territory and set up their mission," Kimberly McKinney said. "I can only imagine that Reverend Marsh must have been in a terrible condition for them to make the decision to turn back."

"I don't like that man, Mr. Temple," Beth Gordon said. "He seems a very mean sort."

"I don't like the way Mr. Rimmer looks at the women and the girls in this company," Abigail McKinney added in. "I've several times caught him looking at my sister in a way that makes me feel uncomfortable. I think he's a lustful man, and she in mourning for her husband."

They'd finished supper and the women had come together near the McKinneys' wagons to enjoy the coolness of the evening before the sun set and the night started to turn cold. Among the other women there, Jefferson Pilcher's wife joined them, as well as Gloria Barnes. Betty Carlisle, Abigail's mother, sat with them on a camp chair. Sophie Bloom, Abigail's sister, was not with them. Since the death of her husband, she had kept mostly to herself with her children. She fed Cody Page, the man who was driving her wagon, and cheerfully talked with him during the days. The other women had also noticed that Mr. Page made his camp near to Sophie's wagon every night.

"I do not like the way Mr. Rimmer looks at women, either," Gloria Barnes said, and the bite in her voice reminded all the women instantly that Gloria Barnes's daughter had been murdered by one of the men associated with Rimmer.

"They are a bunch of ruffians," Mrs. Pilcher said. "The whole lot of them, and Mr. Townes should be ashamed of himself for foisting them upon our company."

"I think so, too," Abigail McKinney said. "I am very surprised at Mr. Townes. All the way to Bridger's Fort, he seemed such a capable man, and I took great comfort in having him as our leader. But since we left that fort, we've lost my poor brother-in-law and Mrs. Barnes's daughter, and my husband tells me that we are in real danger of not clearing the Blue Mountains before snow. It seems we have disaster looming, and I am less confident in Mr. Townes."

"We had to find a guide," Kimberly McKinney said reasonably. "My husband, Wiser, puts a lot of stock in Mr. Townes, and in his brother. And, of course, I trust my husband's judgment. Mr. Townes can't be blamed for what happened to Noah. That was an accident."

"Oh, Solomon also puts stock in Mr. Townes," Abigail said quickly. "And I don't mean to diminish the man's capability. My concern is with Mr. Rimmer and his bunch."

"They're not trustworthy," Beth Gordon said. "And I do not like them at all. I think Mr. Temple may have done something terrible to Reverend and Mrs. Marsh."

Two or three of the women drew a sharp breath at the accusation.

"Let's not have any more talk like that," Wiser McKinney said, walking to where the women had gathered. He'd heard enough of it to get the gist of the conversation. "Mr. Townes had to find a guide who could get us to Oregon City, especially if we fear that we'll encounter bad weather. And he was limited to a choice of Mr. Rimmer or no one. 'A whisperer separates good friends,' ladies. And for the rest of our lives we will look back on our time together as the greatest adventure. Let our memories not be marred by corrupting talk."

"Yes, Mr. McKinney," Kimberly McKinney said. "You're right, of course. But may I ask your opinion of Mr. Rimmer?"

Wiser McKinney smiled and gave his wife a small kiss on the cheek.

"Darling, I will offer an opinion on the man when we are in Oregon City and I can fully judge in what condition we arrived in that place."

Kimberly McKinney smiled at her husband and touched him on his bristly chin. Then she said what she always said when he offered moral discourse.

"You are aptly named, Mr. McKinney."

At the wagons nearest the Snake River, the two wagons toting Elias Townes's possessions, Elias and his brother, Rimmer, and several other men sat smoking their pipes or sharpening knives on stones or whatever they did while they discussed their plans for the morning.

"I saw a couple of willow trees of decent size when I rode the bank earlier," Zeke said. "If we want to fashion a raft, we can get a good one from those. I don't know that we'll find trees enough to get two rafts."

"That's fine," Elias said. "You take the Cody and Jerry and the other boys down the river and make a raft. You can float it back upstream to us."

"Okay."

"Plan to ride out at first light. We can start getting the first wagons ready to move across the river. What does it look like down at the falls?"

"Several drops over big rocks," Zeke said. "I think all the big drops are about six to eight feet. If a wagon gets loose, it'll be dashed on those rocks, though. The river channel narrows and the water runs through there pretty violently. If a wagon goes, it'll be a disaster."

"Put a line on the wagons as we send them across," Rimmer said. "That way none of them get away from us."

Elias nodded his head.

"I'll take my wagon across first," Elias said.

"I should be in the first wagon to go across," Rimmer said. "That way I can help to manage things on the far side."

"That's fine. You and I can go in my wagon."

"Maybe you should put someone else in the wagon with me," Rimmer. "That way you're on the bank here to oversee things on this side."

"I can take the wagon across with Mr. Rimmer," Christian said.

Christian was Elias's younger son. His older boy, Gabe, had been driving wagons on his own and was heavily involved in doing the work to keep the wagon train running. Christian had done less, though he'd pitched in where he could. Elias knew the boy wanted to do more.

"That water runs swift, Chris," Elias said.

"I can handle it," his son answered.

Elias looked at Rimmer.

"I don't see no reason why he can't handle it with me," Rimmer said. "If we go in the water, boy, you just grab hold to the wagon."

Elias felt a pit in his stomach as he considered his son going in the first wagon.

"If you miss the wagon, swim with the flow of the river, making for the bank the whole way. Don't try to fight against the current. Swim with it, but make for the bank." Elias looked around at the other men. He gave Christian's hair an aggressive tussle. "I guess someone will have to distract my wife when Chris gets in the first wagon to go across."

16

RIMMER, LEANING HIS KNEES against the wall of the wagon, raised his pole and thrust it hard into the water. Immediately, the wagon thudded into the pole, the heavy current pushing it hard down stream.

"I'm caught!" Rimmer shouted.

Henry Temple tightened his grip on the rope. Elias and Jeff Pilcher also held the rope, in front of Temple. And Henry Blair had it, almost with his toes in the river.

"Push it hard, Chris!" Elias shouted.

Even though he could not see the rock, Elias knew it was there. The last thing he said to Rimmer and Christian both – right before they'd pushed the wagon down into the river – was to watch out for the rock in the center of the river. The top of the rock wasn't exposed, but from the bank they could see the way the water curled over, white waves splashing just beyond it, and they knew the rock had to be near the surface. They also knew it had to be a sizable rock, big enough that if the wagon lodged against it, the current would spill the wagon completely over. And now, Rimmer's pole was caught between the wagon bed and, somewhere under water, the rock. It was twisting the wagon around, and in a moment the wagon would lodge against that rock.

Rimmer jerked against the pole. He stepped up on something to try to get a better angle to wrench it free.

They heard the collision as the wagon struck the rock and then it didn't move. Stuck there, sideways in the river, the water rushing against it, pushing hard.

"Pull it off the rock!" Rimmer shouted.

Stuck against the rock, the wagon bed began to roll as the current ran under it, dipping precariously down toward the water rushing at it. In a moment, the water would roll the wagon bed under itself, exposing the open top to the flow of the water. It would swamp, and the two men inside would be thrown out.

"Pull!" Henry Temple called to the other men on the rope.

"Wait, no!" Elias shouted. But he was too late to stop them. The rope was taut. The men eager to do something to help, the heaved against the rope, pulling hard up the bank. That one good pull of the rope was all it took. The already precarious wagon bed, tilting hard toward the river, gave the rest of the way. The water rushed into the wagon bed, and the wagon flipped, tossing its occupants.

Seeing the two men go into the water, women along the bank began to scream. Men were shouting. And in the chaos, Elias fixed his eyes on the spot where he last saw his son submerge into the water.

Now free of the rock and upside down, the wagon was like an anchor, pulling the men holding the rope. Henry Blair fell at the water's edge, losing his grip on the rope. Henry Temple simply released it, leaving Elias and Pilcher to try to control the wagon or save it. But it was being swept down the river now, and there was nothing they could do to prevent the wagon from going toward the falls.

"Christian!" Elias shouted, and he didn't worry about the wagon. "Swim! Swim to the bank!"

Elias was running now, along the bank, shouting for his son to swim toward the bank. He saw Christian come up, his arms waving. The wagon was right there beside him, and Christian grabbed it and clutched to it, riding it as the river began to narrow. The wagon was going faster now, and it was leaving Elias behind.

"Let it go!" he shouted to his son. "Get in the river and swim for the bank!"

Downstream, Elias could see the men working on the raft. They'd cut down two willow trees and were busy skinning them of branches. He shouted at the men, but they were nearer to the falls and the noise of the rapids drowned out his shouts.

"Zeke!" Elias called. And he shouted again to Christian to swim for the bank.

Neil Rimmer was on his hands and knees now, exhausted and coughing water onto the bank. He'd swum ashore twenty yards farther down the bank than Elias had come. The water had carried them so far so fast. Elias glanced back over his shoulder. Several people from the wagons were rushing along the bank. He could see Madeline and Gabriel running up on the bluff. He'd run fifty yards or more down the bank, and in that time the wagon bed – and Chris – had swept downriver well ahead of him.

Elias ran past Rimmer without a word to the man.

"SOMETHING'S WRONG," CODY PAGE said.

"What's that?" Zeke said. He had an ax in his hand and was working to remove the branches from the willow. He looked up now and didn't have to wonder at what had happened. It was plain enough what had happened, even if it wasn't clear how.

"That wagon is coming fast," Zeke said.

"Someone's on it," Cody said.

"Damn, Zeke. He's right. That's your nephew holding to the side of the wagon."

"Uh-huh," Zeke said. "Cody, grab me that rope."

They'd brought a rope with them so that they could tow the raft back upstream to the crossing. It was coiled up, and Zeke took the rope from Cody and held it over his head, even as he walked out onto a boulder jutting out over the edge of the river. He waved the rope back and forth, trying to get Christian's attention.

"Run down that way. Meet him halfway. Tell him to let go of that damn wagon and swim for the bank," Zeke said. "If he hangs on to that, it'll be his casket going over the falls."

Jerry Bennett moved first, running as fast as he could and stumbling over the loose rock along the riverbank. He shouted the whole way, calling to Christian to let go of the wagon and swim for the bank. And then the wagon was within thirty yards of him. And Jerry could see the fear in Christian's eyes as the water splashed up into his face and he spluttered.

"Let go of that wagon!" Jerry shouted. "Swim for the bank. Your uncle's going to throw you a rope!"

He shouted the instructions at the boy, and the wagon passed him by and Christian still clung to the upside down wagon.

Jerry could see Elias running toward him, and the wagon was already past, moving quickly toward Zeke and them. Jerry Bennett had never known a time when he felt so helpless. All he could was run back down the bank toward Zeke and the others.

Standing on the big rock, with the water actually cutting below it, Zeke was out as far as he could get without being in the water. Jerry watched him as he tested the weight of the rope, trying to judge the distance. Every man who could see what was happening knew that Zeke would get one throw with that rope. But it didn't matter if Christian Townes didn't turn loose of the wagon. If he held onto the wagon, even a perfect throw of the rope wouldn't save him.

"Turn loose of that damn wagon!" Zeke shouted.

The boy's eyes were fixed on his uncle. And now he let go of the wagon. The water dragged him under at first, but then his head and shoulders reappeared above the surface. The current was pushing him to the far side of the river where the channel narrowed and fell through the rocky shoals and over the falls. Zeke gave the rope a swing with his arm without releasing it, and then another, trying to judge the timing.

On the third swing he flung the rope out over the water.

Christian was gulping water, and though he tried to swim, the current and the weight of his clothes kept pulling him down. He could fight to keep his head above the surface or he could fight to swim for the bank, but he could not do both.

The rope uncoiled in the air. There was a poetry in the way it flew out, unwrapping itself like a whip cutting the sky.

Jerry Bennett stopped running to watch.

Cody Page held his breath.

Zeke watched as the rope slapped down against the water, falling right over the boy's body.

Christian's arms flailed frantically at the rope. His fingers clutched it. Zeke felt his weight pull against the rope, and Zeke leaned back keeping his balance despite the weight dragging him forward.

"Just hang on!" Zeke shouted, no idea if Christian could even hear him.

The rope went taut. The current kept dragging Christian downstream. But at the end of the rope, he now swung toward the bank.

"Run down there and help him," Zeke said.

Zeke just held the rope and let the current do the work. He was the pivot and Christian the pendulum.

Cody and his brother Will rushed down the bank, both of them with branches from one of the willow trees they'd cut down. Cody reached his branch out, and Christian grabbed it with one hand, still holding the rope with the other. Will held Cody to keep him from going in, and when they had the boy over near the bank, Will let go of Cody and reached down and grabbed Christian by the wrist.

As they pulled him over, Zeke looked downstream in time to see the wagon hit the first of the big rocks in the shoals. Boards split. The wagon spun into the heaviest of the water, and then it dropped over the first fall. Zeke lost sight of it for a moment as it went over the fall, but when it reappeared on the other side, it came out in pieces. Zeke recognized a chair as it bashed against another rock. About a third of the wagon dropped down over the next fall, but everything else went in unrecognizable pieces. A board here, a dress there, a water barrel still intact.

Christian was on his back, lying against the rocks on the bank, coughing but alive.

Zeke started reeling in his rope, winding it over his forearm as he did, and he walked along the bank toward his nephew.

"Chris," Zeke said with a chuckle. "You're supposed to float that wagon to the other side of the river, not ride it all the way to Oregon City."

Christian gave him a sour look. His eyes were full of water. Maybe from the river. Maybe tears. The boy was soaking from head to toe. He looked pitiful.

"It wasn't my fault, Uncle Zeke."

Zeke started to say something, but Elias now came running past. He fell on his knees beside his son and dragged the boy up into a bear hug.

17

"TELL ME ABOUT THE southern route," Elias said.

Neil Rimmer nodded his head and used a bandanna to wipe his face. His britches were soaked through. He'd laid out his shirt on some sagebrush to let it dry in the sun. And then he went into it. A little dryer than going north of the Snake River. Water for the livestock was tougher to get to in some places. The route was a shade longer, maybe it was add four or five days to their journey. But it required no crossings of the Snake River.

"Why is it not the preferred route?" Elias asked.

"Honestly, I couldn't say. It's an old Injun trail. So far as I know, only the old trappers know about it."

Whatever happened, they'd lost this day.

The people who elected Elias Townes to lead them to Oregon City were gathered up on the bluff overlooking the river. Elias and a few others were down near the bank. The undercarriage of his wagon still sat there on the bank, waiting for a raft to take it across the Snake River. But that journey wouldn't happen now, and the undercarriage of Elias's wagon had reached the end of its travels.

Zeke and some of the others had walked downstream, down below the falls, to see if they could salvage anything from Elias's wagon.

Maddie sat with her younger son, having wrapped him in a blanket, and she refused to let him out of her sight.

Gabriel unhelpfully spent half an hour lecturing Christian about how he should have swam toward the bank and never should have grabbed onto the wagon bed.

Elias, the fear for his son subsided now, had another overwhelming thought that he did not say out loud to Neil Rimmer. The strong box he carried in his wagon. There were three strongboxes, each one nailed to the bed of three of the wagons. One in Elias's wagon. One in Zeke's wagon. One in the wagon that carried their equipment to start their new business in Oregon Territory. Those strongboxes each held a third of the money – the money Elias collected from the other emigrants in the company to buy into the trek. This was the money Elias would use to pay the wages of the hired hands. His own men – Jerry Bennett and the Page brothers and the Tucker brothers and Caleb Driscoll – and Henry Blair, the guide he hired to get the party as far as Bridger's Fort, and Rimmer and his men. It was money for supplies along the trail. It was also the money Elias and Zeke brought with them that would get them through their first winter in the new territory and allow them to start their business.

Elias needed that money.

But he also knew that there was no way he was getting the other emigrants in his party to agree to a river crossing here, and that was another problem that had to be dealt with.

"They all saw how fast that wagon went downstream and over the falls," Elias said with a nod at the people gathered up on the bluff. "They're thinking about their possessions, and their lives."

Rimmer nodded.

"I can only offer you my best advice, Mr. Townes," Rimmer said. "This here, with that wagon, it was what you call a fluke. My damn pole got lodged. The wagon hit that rock just right. If we'd had one other man in the wagon with a pole, we'd have gotten across without a problem, and I suppose it was my fault for not thinking we needed three men to float the wagon across. You let me, and I'll get all the rest of these wagons across here without any more trouble. That's my best advice."

"I think we'll have a mutiny if we try to cross here," Elias said. "Some of those women in our party are hard-headed, and some of their men are weak-willed."

"I've found in my life those two things go hand-in-hand," Rimmer chuckled.

"If we can't cross here, what's your next best advice."

"My next best advice is to cross at three islands. But you can plan for the water to be just as swift. If they don't want to cross here, they won't want to cross at three islands."

"I think that's true. So the southern route?"

"We can go the southern route," Rimmer said, sounding almost resigned to the idea that he didn't have any choice in the matter. "It's not preferable, but we can sure do it."

Elias nodded his head.

"All right, then, Mr. Rimmer. I think you should make plans to guide us on the southern route."

"Roll out in the morning?" Rimmer said.

Elias shook his head.

"Head them out now. Every wagon that is ready to leave now, go on and take them."

Rimmer looked downstream toward the falls.

"You've got six or seven men scattered on the riverbank. Shouldn't we wait for them?"

"We'll catch up," Elias said. "Probably tomorrow. I want to see what we can salvage from my wrecked wagon, but I don't want everyone else to be stuck waiting."

"All right," Rimmer said. "If that's how you want to do it."

Elias went up the bluff and talked to some of the other men and then addressed the party as a whole.

"The main body of the wagon train is going to roll out now," he said. "After talking with Mr. Rimmer, I've decided it's best that we take another route and avoid crossing the Snake River."

A few of the women breathed relief at that. Three or four of the men clapped their hands.

"We're going to take a southern route that keeps us on the south side of the Snake River the whole way. We'll pick up the main route of the trail near Fort Boise."

They'd all witnessed the destruction of Elias's wagon. Fearing for their own property, and their lives, no one argued about making the journey along the southern route. And in truth, no one was in a position to. The only man who knew what to expect from any of the various options was Rimmer. For the rest of them, one way was just as good or bad as another way. Except now they feared the river most of all, and the southern route allowed them to avoid crossing the river.

"This was you're looking for?" Jerry Bennett said, hauling up a box lodged against some rocks.

"That's it," Zeke said, and all of the men nearby could hear the relief in his voice.

They'd recovered a dress and a shirt and a pair of britches. A quilt that so full of water that Zeke swore it weighed close to twenty pounds. They found a smashed up lantern. The water barrel was busted all to hell. The wagon seat was intact, for all the good that did. The sack of sugar was all spilled out and the flour was ruined, but Zeke fetched out a sack of coffee beans, figuring those could dry and still be put to good use. They found an ax in good shape, still, but Elias's entire keg of nails was gone.

As soon as Jerry Bennett hefted the strong box out of the water, Zeke was ready to give up the search. Everything else was replaceable, especially now that they had the box.

The box was still nailed to a piece of the floor of the wagon, and Zeke pried that loose. The box was heavy, and Cody and Zeke and Henry Blair took turns toting it back upstream, maneuvering over the rocks, climbing the hills.

"What do you think, Mr. Zeke," Henry Blair said. "Should we cross here or try it somewhere else?"

"I don't know, Henry," Zeke said. "Before we came down here hunting this box, even while Christian was still coughing out some of the Snake River he swallowed, Elias had folks in his ear urging him to find an alternative to the crossing. My guess is we won't make the crossing."

"But should we?" Henry persisted.

Zeke glanced around to see if the others would hear him. Cody was nearby, but Jerry and Will Page and Billy and Johnny Tucker had walked on a ways ahead.

"I think we should go on and cross the river here, Henry," Zeke said. "Me and these boys, we all grew up on the Ohio River. We can move a wagon bed across the river without any trouble. Even a fast moving river like this one today. Mr. Rimmer ought to have been able to do it. Honestly, it perplexes me how it was even so much of a problem for him. But we could make the crossing here, and we wouldn't lose another wagon. My instinct tells me that if this is where other wagon trains ahead of us have crossed, then we should cross here. Or we should go to the three island crossing farther on. That's where Elias's brochure says we should cross. And I think we should cross there. But some of the men in this company are led by the whims of their wives, and some of those women make decisions based on what they're afraid of, not what makes the most sense. So I reckon when we get back, they'll tell us they've decided to go on with this southern route."

"I think we should we should cross here, too," Henry said. "I heard Rimmer say that there aren't even any tracks going that southern route. Nothing to follow to know for sure we're on the right path, going the best way. We'll have to figure out for ourselves where the best water is. When we cross a creek or go through a canyon of any kind, we'll have to pick out the best route on our own."

"Maybe we should try to talk Mr. Townes into crossing here," Cody suggested. "Here, Zeke. Tote this box for me."

"Yep," Zeke said, and he hefted the box up onto his shoulder and toted it for the next hundred yards.

When they finally got back to the bluffs, they saw they were too late to suggest that they should try the crossing again. Zeke even decided that he would offer to take his wagon across next. But most of the wagons were gone from the bluffs.

"I've sent them on," Elias explained. "I'm worried about the time we're going to lose. I figure a few of us can catch up to the main group without any problem."

"Sure," Zeke said. And he decided not to mention his thoughts about making the river crossing.

The few bits of Elias's personal possessions that could salvaged they loaded into the tool wagon, as Elias called it.

Marie already began finding things she could loan to Madeline, but Maddie's chief worry was provisions. How could they make it another five or six hundred miles through the wilderness without sufficient food?

"Of course, we will share everything we have," Marie assured her.

Elias had also put beans and rice and flour and an entire slab of bacon in the other wagon, the one with all the tools in it. It wouldn't be sufficient to get them the rest of the way, but it would help considerably.

"And you've shared so many meals with us that we have plenty," Josie Tucker said.

It was true that Madeline had often fed the entire group of hired hands, including Billy Tucker's wife Josie and Johnny Tucker's wife Anna.

"Everyone will share with you," Anna Tucker said.

Cody Page was driving Sophie Bloom's wagon, so the pregnant widow and her children had stayed back when the rest of the wagon train set out. Zeke's wagon was there, and Elias's second wagon, and the wagon that the Tuckers shared with the other hired hands. None of them brought much, other than provisions and clothes. They would rely on Elias and Zeke to help them get settled through their first winter in the territory. None of them had much back in Kentucky, so they didn't bring much.

The only immediate member of the Townes group who did not stay back was Elias's oldest daughter. Maggie Winter and her new husband Jason had gone on ahead with the others.

As the sun set and the small group spent their second night in the bluffs over the Snake River crossing, Zeke wished that Maggie and Jason hadn't gone along. If they'd stayed back, too, maybe the Townes folks could just cross the river and move on without all those other emigrants. Zeke felt the others were a drag. Alone, they could have made faster time and run into fewer troubles.

What worried him was the troubles that still lay ahead.

But Maddie and Elias would never agree to crossing the river without their oldest daughter and her husband. So it was a simple imagining. Zeke didn't even bring it up to Marie.

The smaller group spent the night there on the bluffs above the Snake River crossing.

At sunup, they got moving. They went quickly with only the oxen hitched to their wagons and their saddle horses, they were not slowed by an abundance of livestock.

They followed the tracks of the many wagon trains that had come before them, and those tracks followed the Snake River.

What Elias and Zeke did not realize was that the the Snake River here made one of its many wide bends to the northeast and then curved back to flow to the west. It was there, where the river flowed to the west again, that the three island crossing could be found.

Rimmer, though, had straightened the curve. He'd left the worn path – probably deciding that they would leave it anyway, so why not sooner rather than later – and set out using his own dead reckoning as his guide. He figured to save maybe fifteen or twenty miles, a full day's ride.

So on their first day trying to catch up to the main body of the wagon train, Elias's smaller group still had not caught up with the others. It was perplexing to him, but not worrying. They'd simply had a good day of travel. On the second day of trying to catch up, Elias's smaller group camped a third night without the main group.

On the third day, they came to the three island crossing.

They wouldn't have known it except that here the tracks stopped.

Shoshone Indians camped here tried to encourage them to go back to the crossing. Some even ran ahead of the wagons and waved their hands and pointed back. Elias and Zeke tried to make them understand that they were trying to catch other wagons, but the Indians only had a little English and neither Elias nor Zeke had any of the Native People's language.

At last the Indians let them go, but their urgency at trying to get the Townes brothers to turn around left both men feeling uncertain.

Zeke did ride down to the crossing, to see the three islands for himself. The river ran swift, but the crossing looked easy enough. He rejoined his brother convinced they could have easily made the crossing and that the salmon falls crossing had been a mistake to try.

Finally, five days after losing Elias's wagon, the Townes brothers caught up to the main body of the wagon train. Had they not spotted them from a high hill, they might have gone right on past without ever knowing it. Neil Rimmer had led the wagon train not only far off the beaten path, but now he had them far below the Snake River. Elias thought they should have been no more than four miles south of the river. They were actually about ten miles away from the river, so far that Rimmer or one of the others had to periodically ride north, away from the wagon train, just to check on their position in relation to the only landmark.

What struck Zeke, right from the moment they caught the wagon train, was how dry and dusty it suddenly was. The sage grew in patches and there was no grass. Just hard-packed sand and rock.

18

"MR. TOWNES, I HAVE an issue I need to speak to you about," Wiser McKinney said.

"Certainly, Mr. McKinney," Elias said. "Privately?"

Already they were speaking privately. No one was around at all. Elias stood by his wagon, loaded with tools, that remained at the front of the column of wagons. But his wife and his family were all back at Zeke's wagon now. Since losing their own, Maddie and the girls had fallen in with Zeke's wife. They spent almost all their time at the back of the wagon train, unless the girls were helping with some of the children in the party. But Madeline had leaned heavily on Marie, grateful for a sympathetic friend, and also grateful at Marie's generosity in sharing provisions.

None of the other emigrants at the nearby wagons were close enough to hear anything from their conversation. Nevertheless, Elias and Wiser walked some distance away from the camp.

"What's the problem, Mr. McKinney?"

"It's Mr. Rimmer," Wiser said.

"What about him?"

"I hesitate to say anything, but I've been appointed to voice the concern."

Elias waited, but Wiser McKinney did not say anything. He seemed to be searching for the best way to say what was on his mind.

"Say what you've come to say," Elias said.

Wiser nodded his head and steeled his resolve.

"The women have expressed concerns and, like I said, they asked me to make their complaints known to you. Mr. Rimmer and some of his men are making the women nervous."

Elias sighed heavily.

"Mr. McKinney," Elias said, but then he stopped himself. He wanted to tell Wiser that he shouldn't allow himself to be embroiled in the plots of gossipy women. But Elias stopped from saying it. His association with these people was temporary – though after more than a thousand miles of sharing the trial with them, Elias felt that the other emigrants were his new family, his new hometown. He could imagine himself, in the future, when asked where he was from answering that he was from the Trail and that the McKinneys and the Barneses were his neighbors. And Elias reminded himself now that he had been raised to bear his neighbors' burdens. "Nervous in what way, Mr. McKinney?"

"The women say that Rimmer and his men look at them with lustful intent."

Elias chuckled, but immediately regretted it.

"It's not a joke, Mr. Townes," Wiser said. "They take it very seriously. They are uncomfortable around these men, and it is a universal feeling."

"Is it?" Elias said. "Universal?"

"It is. Not only that, Mr. Brown believes that one of Mr. Rimmer's men might have been sneaking around his wagon in the middle of the night."

Elias narrowed his eyes.

"Wiser, Mr. Brown also thought he had a rattlesnake near his wagon and so shot his own boots in the middle of the night."

Wiser chuckled and nodded his head.

"Yes, Mr. Townes. Indeed he did. But we were without you for five days. The attitude around camp very quickly changed when you were not among us. Mr. Rimmer and his men treated all of us as if we were a military column

– ordering us what to do, unwilling to receive advice. And it was they who kept the night watch. They accepted no help from the rest of us, which I found to be very odd. They insisted that the livestock be kept closer to the camp, thus disturbing everyone's sleep."

Elias held up a hand.

"All right, Mr. McKinney," he said. "Is this a general complaint about Mr. Rimmer and his treatment of you while I was gone, or is this a specific complaint about how he looks at the women."

Wiser shrugged his shoulders and nodded his head from side to side.

"I suppose it's too much of both," Wiser said. "We have general complaints about Mr. Rimmer. But the women have specific complaints. And also, we all worry that he has no idea where we're going. We've left a fertile valley for a desert."

Elias nodded his head. Kimberly McKinney was coming toward them and was within earshot now.

"On that note, Mr. McKinney, I share your concern. Mr. Rimmer did tell me it was dryer this way, less forage. I did not imagine it would be so dry and no forage. I'll watch Rimmer and his men. If I think they're being untoward with the women, I'll say something to him. Is that fair?"

"Mr. Townes, I don't mean to add to your troubles. And I should tell you, that my husband comes to you only after much debate with me and some of the other women. But this thing with Mr. Rimmer and his men, it is very real. A woman has an instinct about these things. She knows when a man looks at her like a lion looks at a lamb. I assure you. And if you don't think so, ask Mrs. Townes. Some of the women are mildly concerned. But some of the women are truly terrified of Mr. Rimmer and his men."

Elias could see the sincerity on her face, he could hear the earnest plea in her voice. He wasn't sure what she expected him to do about it. But no doubt, Wiser McKinney's wife, at least, was truly afraid.

Wiser and his wife brought this to Elias on the evening of the day that the two groups came back together.

The next day, Rimmer came with a more urgent matter.

"WE LACK SUFFICIENT GRASS," Neil Rimmer said. "The animals can't forage."

"So I've noticed," Elias said.

Gabriel drove the front wagon, currently sitting on the driver's seat with Christian sitting there beside him. Billy Tucker came along behind them in the second wagon. Billy was walking along with his team, and his wife, Josie, was riding in the driver's seat, resting in the shade under the canvas.

When Rimmer caught up to him, Elias was walking up at the front of the wagons. He'd turned Tuckee loose with the remuda and had a different horse today. But he'd just let the horse walk with the wagon. He'd not even saddled that horse.

"I'm wondering if it makes sense to break up the wagon train into two separate groups with two separate cow columns," Rimmer said. "Keep a couple of miles apart, one farther to the south. That way we've got more ground for the livestock to graze, especially at camp."

Elias gave Rimmer a hard look. Rimmer was mounted on a bay gelding that had come from Elias's remuda.

"I wonder at the wisdom of dividing the party when we've ventured out into seldom traveled territory," Elias said. "I already have it in mind that we may be more exposed here to Indian attack than we would be on the beaten path. And if we separate ourselves, even by just a couple of miles, do we not invite marauders to try to cut out some of our cattle and horses?"

Rimmer nodded his head.

"That could certainly be a risk," he said. "Of course, if the cattle and horses are all dead, it hardly makes a difference."

"Uh-huh," Elias said. "What about water, Mr. Rimmer? The Snake River is exceedingly difficult to get to here."

"There's places where it's easier to get at here," Rimmer said.

"But we're traveling half a day's ride from the river already," Elias said. "I'm afraid we've wandered into more difficulty than I realized."

"Well, I did tell you that the water and forage would be tougher to come by if we took the southern route," Rimmer said. "That decision was left to you."

Elias tucked his top lip under his bottom teeth and bit. In that way, he knew he wouldn't make any rash statement. But in his mind, everything was rash.

"For now, Mr. Rimmer, I think it's best that we do not separate the wagon train. I'll consider it as we go, but I think it would be a mistake. If disaster strikes, I feel like it would be better for all of us to endure it together than to face disaster separately."

"You're in charge, Mr. Townes," Rimmer said, a dismissive tone in his voice. Rimmer wheeled his horse and started toward the back of the wagon train. Elias figured he was moving back to the cow column.

Up ahead, a mile or farther, Elias could see Zeke's silhouette sitting atop the big gray horse he preferred. Zeke had ridden forward to look for a good place to camp. Water had been Elias's chief criteria, but he doubted that Zeke would find water.

They were only a few miles south of the Snake River, but the countryside here had become extremely dry, and it had happened overnight. Seeing the state of things here, Elias didn't have to wonder at why the emigrants ahead of him had risked those river crossings to avoid this country. This was a bad route to the Oregon Territory. Rimmer's cautions about this route had been mild, softened. For what purpose, Elias couldn't imagine. The man had forced himself into just as bad a situation as the rest of them were in. It served no purpose that would benefit Rimmer.

"Maybe when he came through here it was a particularly wet season," Zeke said when the two of them talked about it later that day at camp. Zeke wasn't as much offering to give Rimmer the benefit of the doubt as he was looking for different possibilities.

"You don't believe that," Elias said.

"No. I don't believe that. What I believe is that I trust the man less with every day that I know him."

Elias winced.

"I feel the same way about him. Bridger vouched for him. If he'd not, I wouldn't have hired him on."

"We probably shouldn't have ever left out of St. Jo without a guide who could lead us the whole way," Zeke said. "But we made the best choices we could in the moment. You've got all these folks, a hundred of them, looking at you to get them to the Northwest Territory. You can't get angry with yourself now for making the decisions that seemed best at the time."

"I'm afraid I'm going to have to make another decision soon," Elias said.

"About Rimmer?" Zeke said.

Elias told Zeke what Rimmer had said about breaking up the wagon train into two columns.

"What purpose does that serve, Zeke?"

Zeke shrugged.

"Well, Rimmer told you it would spread out the livestock. It would do that."

"What other purpose?" Elias said. "What's the first thing that comes to mind for you when I say that Rimmer wants to split the wagon train into two columns separated my miles?"

"He wants to get some of us away from the others because if we're separated into two columns it would be easier for him and his men to prey upon one and then the other."

Elias nodded his head, glancing around to be sure no one had overheard their conversation.

"That's exactly my thought, too."

LOOSE ROCKS KICKED FREE from the narrow ledge and dropped down a hundred feet or more.

Though signs suggested others had come this way before, no one could defend calling this a path. It was just a narrow ledge, a rocky ledge, and it dropped at a slope not too steep for the horses and oxen. Once the men got them down the first forty or fifty feet, the ledge opened some into a draw. There, the precarious drop disappeared. But those first forty-five feet, it was enough to make a man's blood run cold in the heat of August.

"Careful. That damn steer keeps wanting to veer off the side," Elias called to Jerry Bennett who had a rope over the steer's head and was urging him down. "Jerry, if he loses his footing, he might panic and do any damn thing. You be ready to get out of his way if he comes running."

Jerry laughed. He was five feet in front of the steer, standing on a narrow ledge with a hundred foot vertical drop to one side and a wall of basalt rock to the other side.

"Not sure where you want me to go, Mr. Townes!"

"I wouldn't go over the side," Elias said. "And I wouldn't want to press against that wall and get caught between the steer and the wall. Maybe you could jump his head, land on his back, and ride him down?"

That drew some laughter from a lot of the men watching. Jerry grinned and licked the sweat off his upper lip.

Elias kneeled at the rim of the Snake River canyon, one knee firmly planted against the rock. It made his head swim to look down over the scene like this.

A half dozen cows followed the steer, brave enough to go without being dragged down if they could see the steer go first. It was slow, tedious work, and yet every man felt his heart pound in his chest.

"Just go easy Jerry," Zeke said. Zeke was down at the draw where there was a little more room to work, waiting for Jerry to get the steer that far down.

The steer didn't want to go. His big eyes bulged in his head, and he kept looking at the open space below him. Jerry tugged on the rope and got another couple of steps from the steer.

This was how they had to water the livestock. Bring them down into the river gorge in sixes and eights and tens. Lead them step by step. Throw buckets of water on them and wash them down while they drank. And pray none of them decided to break into a run.

Just watering the animals was the chore of an afternoon. They'd gone four miles today when Henry Blair, riding ahead along the river, saw this path they could use to take the animals down. It had been like this for three or four days now. Making distance on the trail wasn't nearly as vital to their immediate survival as finding a spot where they could get the livestock down to the river. There was no other water – no creeks or rivers feeding into the Snake, no pools or springs.

They had four men riding in advance of the column of wagons. Henry Blair, Zeke, Rimmer's man Bowdon, and Captain Walker. The four of them rode separately, leap-frogging each other along the rim, all searching for a spot where they could make a stop for water.

Elias shook his head as he glanced down into the gorge where they already had thirty oxen and a dozen horses.

Jeff Pilcher and Caleb Driscoll were down in the gorge overseeing the watering of the livestock, making sure all of the animals were sufficiently watered and washed.

Gabriel and Christian and some of the other boys from the wagon train had fishing poles and were catching supper from the river. They'd already pulled a fair number of good sized trout from the river. But Elias would have preferred that they were down there watering the livestock. This was a chore that had to be finished before dark. He couldn't have men leading horses and cattle up a precarious path without sufficient light to see.

Rimmer acted as if this was all to be expected. But Elias felt duped.

"I told you there would be less water this way," Rimmer would respond anytime Elias broached the subject. But what good was it to talk about it? They could not now change a thing. They couldn't go back to the crossings. They couldn't argue enough water onto the dry and dusty prairie.

19

INCLUDING NEIL RIMMER HIMSELF, there were now just the five of them.

Norwood, sacrificed for Rimmer's sins. Hayton, done-in by Henry Temple.

He still had Bowdon, who was a solid man in a fight. Rimmer had seen Bowdon in a fight with some Injuns, and he'd killed three of them with his knife. Any man who could put down three Injuns with a knife was a man worth his salt. What Henry Temple lacked in youthful agility he made up for in strength and meanness. It didn't take Henry long to get worked up into a killing temper, and when he was there, he worked pretty hard at the job.

The other man in the outfit who Rimmer knew pretty well was a freighter called Duhon. They'd traveled together back and forth from the Missouri to the Snake several times.

Less known to him was the man they called Loop Garoo. He was French-Canadian and halfbreed Injun, but that didn't slow him down when it was time to take scalps off them Wind River Injuns. Loop Garoo, who said his name meant wolf in French, was a wiry, long-haired man, probably in his mid-thirties. He knew all the old trappers, and Rimmer figured he was as mean as Henry Temple and as good in a fight as Bowdon. But he was also a quiet man.

He made Rimmer a mite nervous, because Rimmer never was sure if Loop Garoo was all the way in with the rest of them or not. He never agreed to a plan. He just didn't disagree with it, neither.

"Townes ain't gonna let us separate the wagon train," Rimmer told the others as they sat around a campfire late at night with no one else around.

"If we can't get the wagons separate, we can't take none of their wagons," Duhon said.

"I think that's right," Rimmer agreed. "If we'd been able to get them separated, we could've sent Townes and his brother and their men with one half of the wagon train and we could've taken the other. And then we could've done what we wanted with them. Brown and Barnes and Pilcher and those men, we could've cut their throats and had their women and their wagons and everything else. But we can't take on every man in this wagon train with just the five of us."

"I don't want take all these greenhorns all the way to Oregon City," Henry Temple growled. "I'm exhausted keeping company with them. I never signed up to work this hard."

"We're working like dogs," Bowdon said. And with a grin at the men around the campfire, he added, "If I'd wanted to work for a living, I would have stayed back east."

"Here's what I'm going to do," Rimmer said. "In the morning, I'm going to tell Townes we want more money to guide them. I'm going to tell him that his decision to come the southern route is making this a bigger chore than any of us signed up for."

Rimmer grinned. He felt that he'd struck upon a bit of genius with his ruse to get Townes onto this southern route. To a point, it was true that trappers and Indians came along this way. Indians had trails all over that not even the trappers knew anything about. But one trapper leading a couple of mules down these narrow ledges to water or trying to find sufficient grazing for two animals was something different altogether from an entire wagon train with forty wagons and a couple hundred four-legged beasts.

Yet Rimmer had arranged it so that Townes could never claim it wasn't his idea to come this way. He'd even flipped that wagon at the crossing. Truth is, he expected Townes's son to go over the falls and get about as smashed up as that wagon did. But as it turned out, nobody had to die to get the women to be too frightened of the crossing. Just seeing that wagon go over was enough to scare them off of it.

"So I'm going to tell Townes he's got to pay us more or we're going back. I figure we can get another fifty dollars a piece off of him. The man is bound for Oregon with plans to start a business. He's got his payroll and his money for a house and every thing else. He's as good as striking gold. Once he hands over the money, we'll slip out in the middle of the night. We can steal whatever we want. And I'm going to work it so that we don't even have to worry about them following us."

It had been such a good plan. And he wanted the others to acknowledge it. He wanted them to remark on his cunning and talk about how glad they were that they'd decided to ride along with him. Hubbard, the man who'd led this outfit before the split, was on his way back to Missouri to sell Injun scalps for ten dollars, and Rimmer and his boys would be headed back to Bridger's Fort in a day or two with money enough to see them through another year or two.

Instead of the acknowledgment Rimmer thought he was due, Bowdon just made a fresh complaint.

"Look here, Rimmer. You told us we'd be able to get at some of these women. Now you're talking about leaving out of here without any of us getting even one of them."

Rimmer chewed his lip for a moment. He wanted to thrash that man.

"You want the women? Didn't I just say we're going to ride out of here and steal anything we want? If you want to steal a girl, you can steal a girl. You just keep right on rolling with my plan."

OFF THEIR LEFT SHOULDERS, the emigrants in the Townes Party could see a small mountain range through the haze of sandy dust blowing out across the wide expanse. Elias figured the range was about twenty or thirty miles to the southwest.

The river now had turned northwest. The rough map in his brochure showed the river's wide bend to the north, and he was guessing that they were probably still five or six days from connecting with the trail at the Boise River. Maybe more than that. Elias had as his guides only rough-drawn maps that at times seemed to be just a guess – and no mention in the brochure at all of a southern route – and Rimmer's reckoning. He had to weigh one against the other, and both had proved so far to be unreliable.

Rimmer was out in front of the wagon train today, scouting the best path. Since leaving the worn trail at the three islands crossing and striking out on their own, someone had to ride in advance to make sure they weren't driving the wagons and cattle directly toward a canyon where they might have to turn around. That was in addition to the people riding along the rim of the Snake River looking for spots where they could water the animals.

The land was flat enough and easy enough to cross that they were making about twelve miles a day. But on the days when they stopped to water the animals, they were lucky to do more than four or five miles. Of course, in addition to those four miles there were probably six or eight miles of walking the livestock to the river and bringing them back. The days when they did the fewest miles were also the days when they worked the hardest.

Elias was probably about two miles in front of the wagon train. He couldn't see the wagons now. They were down in a depression, and hills behind him blocked them from his view. But he could see Rimmer riding back his way at a pretty good lope.

"Mr. Townes! I believe I've found a good spot for us to make camp for the night," Rimmer called as he approached the hill where Elias sat Tuckee.

"Any grass?" Elias called back.

"Not much, but a little," Rimmer said, his horse now mounting the hill. "It's still maybe three miles up ahead of where we are right now, but it'll be a good spot. Sits down in a little valley, so the grass is better than all the dust up here. There's some rocky hills around that will give us a little shade for what's left of the afternoon and maybe a break from the wind.

"What mountains are those?" Elias asked Rimmer.

Rimmer gave a glance off in the direction Elias indicated.

"That's a nice little range of mountains," Rimmer said. "Ain't got no name that I know of. The Owyhee River is on the other side of them, and I've always just called them the Owyhee Mountains. I done some trapping and hunting up in those hills. Good trees, excellent streams running through them. A man on the run could last a long while in those mountains."

"Maybe we should take these animals over there," Elias said. He meant it as a joke, but the truth was the animals were all starting to look skinny, and the chore of watering them had become such a burden that some among the emigrants were actually talking about abandoning their wagons and packing from here.

They sat on the hill for several long moments, both of them watching their backtrail now, waiting for the wagon train to emerge out of the wide depression where they currently snaked their way.

"I don't know if now is the time to say something or not, Mr. Townes, but I think it's going to have to be done."

"About what?" Elias asked.

"Well, me and my men were talking last night, and the boys are getting a little fouled up."

"Fouled up?" Elias said. "How so?"

"They don't think it's fair the amount of work that's being put on them."

Elias grew immediately angry. Typically, Elias could keep calm in the light of problems caused by the men to whom he paid wages. He was well accustomed to strong-willed men who got to talking and deciding something wasn't fair. But so many pressures were on him now, so many burdens that weighed on his shoulders like sacks of boulders.

"Mr. Rimmer, we agreed upon a fair price back at Bridger's Fort. Mr. Bridger vouched for you and your men. If you're coming to me now with a request for more money, I want you to know – before you say another word – that I would consider that tantamount to highway robbery. And I won't be a victim of a gang of thieves."

Rimmer put up a hand.

"Simmer down, Mr. Townes. It's just you and me out here talking. I ain't making demands on you. I'm just telling you what my boys are saying. Coming this way, they're all being called on to work more than they thought they would have to. You got to remember, you're dealing here with freighters and old trappers and men who come out to the wilds of these parts because they ain't sociable. And now they're all having to help some of these greenhorns you got in your wagon train. Every little thing these people need done for them, and they're looking on my men to do them. And it's harder now, on account of your decision to come this southern route. We're having deal with watering these animals and drive them out farther and farther for forage. And then we got them Blue Mountains in front of us yet. I can all but assure you, we're going to run into trouble trying to cross the Blues."

"By trouble, you mean snow?"

"That's exactly what I mean. And all my boys know that when we're trying to get through snow drifts that's three or four feet deep, your greenhorns are going to be shouting for Mr. Rimmer and his boys all the louder than they do even now. You understand me, Mr. Townes? The boys is fed up, and they all know it's going to get worse. Why, the way I see it, the only thing between you folks and starvation is me and my men."

Elias mastered his anger now. He breathed easier. He felt the pounding in his chest get calmer.

"How much?" Elias said.

"It ain't just a question of money," Rimmer said. "The boys, they're seriously talking about packing back to Fort Hall."

"How much?" Elias repeated.

"There's five of us. A hundred dollars a man."

"Five hundred dollars? Paid when we arrive in Oregon City?"

"I don't hardly think they'd go for that," Rimmer said. "Once you're in Oregon City, they might worry you won't pay what you owe. Maybe you'll try to bargain it down to another twenty-five dollars a man."

"In the same way you're trying now to bargain it up to another hundred dollars a man?"

"It's more work than what we signed on for, coming this southern route," Rimmer said. "Of course, I won't abandon you, Mr. Townes. I'll stick. Even if the boys all head for home."

Elias took a heavy breath. He had half a mind right now to draw the Colt saddle gun from its holster and shoot Rimmer in the head. It's what he would have done with any other highwayman who attempted to thieve from him on the trail.

"I can't say I'm not disappointed in you Mr. Rimmer. I took you for an honest man. I feel like you've engineered this scheme, engineered my predicament for your own personal gain. But I'll pay you the money because I've got all these lives depending on me. If it was just you and me out here, we'd part this conversation with a very different outcome."

Rimmer laughed.

"Ain't no call for hostilities between us, Mr. Townes. I understand you're angry, but we've got a long way to go to get to Oregon City. You pay me that five hundred tonight, and I'll divvy out among the men right away. It'll keep them loyal."

"Uh-huh," Elias said. "I'll divvy it out to the men myself. That way, everyone knows it's fair dealings."

Rimmer grinned.

"Fine by me."

ZEKE GRITTED HIS TEETH.

"Brother, please tell me you told him goodbye and good riddance," Zeke said. "I can see the man walking over yonder, so I know you didn't bash his brains out – which is what he deserves. So the only thing I can figure is that you told him to go on and get and good luck at Fort Hall."

Elias shook his head.

"We've got all these people depending on us, Zeke. It would be one thing if it was just us and our families. But Walter Brown over there, with his shot up boots and his teenage daughters. How does he get to Oregon City without Rimmer and his men? Or Sophie Bloom? Her husband dead. Is she going to lead her oxes down the escarpments to the river canyon to water them? Marcus Weiss? If he can't call on Henry Temple for aid –"

"I take your point," Zeke interrupted. "So take up a new collection from the other people. You're talking about the money we've saved – you and me both – to start our lives in the Northwest Territory. And you're going to give it to these men who we do not need. Our boys can do the work. It's Cody who's driving Sophie Bloom's wagon. It's Jerry Bennett and the Tucker brothers who're doing most work to water the livestock. And you and me. And Jeff Pilcher. Rimmer and them are next to useless. If we were back home in Paducah working at the timber mill, you'd have already cashiered them right out. Why does that bunch of shirkers get a pass from you just because we're on the Snake River and not the Ohio?"

"Because that group of shirkers is all we've got on the Snake River," Elias said. "Their knowledge of the lay of the land is what we need them for."

The two of them were shouting now, and they'd drawn the attention of many others around them.

Solomon McKinney came from his campfire where his wife was cooking dinner.

"Mr. Townes? Is everything all right?"

Elias nodded his head.

"It is, Mr. McKinney. Our guides have decided to increase the price on us."

Solomon nodded his head thoughtfully.

"They have led us to a place where their knowledge is more valuable than it was before and renegotiated the deal in their favor," he said. "No one should be surprised. What do you intend to do about it?"

"He's going to pay them," Zeke snapped.

"That does seem to be for the best," Solomon said, adding a nod of support at Elias.

Elias removed from the strongbox that Jerry Bennett rescued from the bottom of the falls a sack of twenty-dollar gold pieces. It pained him to part with the money, but he counted out twenty-five gold pieces. Zeke watched him, and fumed.

"I'll go with you to pay them off," Zeke said.

"You don't have to," Elias said.

"I want to," Zeke said.

And so the two of them went, along with a self-appointed delegation of some of the other men who'd overheard the commotion between the Townes brothers. Along the way, Solomon McKinney suggested that the money be handed over with a stern reproach against further renegotiating of the contractual agreement.

"You can reproach them as stern as you like," Zeke said. "It won't matter none to these men. But I intend to have some words that may make them think twice about it."

Elias put a hand on Zeke's shoulder.

"I'd rather you not. We need their help to get through the Blue Mountains. I don't want you doing something that will jeopardize that."

"Oh, I'll be all right," Zeke said. "I've taken a measure of the man, and I think I've read him pretty well, Elias."

The men found Rimmer and his outfit camped near the livestock. They had a campfire going and one of them was cooking beans and bacon in a pan and boiling rice in a pot.

"Mr. Rimmer, we've brought your additional pay," Elias said, approaching the men.

"You brought a whole contingent to hand it over, I see," Rimmer said.

"The contingent, Mr. Rimmer, is to make certain that we are all in unanimity about our agreement going forward," Solomon McKinney said. "This is the last installment on the wages. You'll help guide us to Oregon City without any further amendments to our bargain."

"Sure," Rimmer said. "You can bet on that."

Zeke plucked the sack from Elias's hands and went up to Henry Temple.

"Mr. Temple, what do we owe you now?" Zeke said.

Rimmer started to intervene, but he realized too late what Zeke was doing.

"Fifty dollars more," Temple said, and Zeke shot a grin at Elias who had intended to hand over five hundred dollars to Rimmer.

"Here's sixty dollars, Mr. Temple. That's what we'll pay all of you."

Rimmer shot a wry smile at Zeke.

"That's fine," he said.

For those who knew that Elias had collected a hundred dollars for each man, it was pretty plain that Rimmer had intended to cheat his friends.

Zeke handed out the money to the men and gave the remainder back to Elias.

"We'll set out at sunup," Elias said.

"That'll be fine," Rimmer agreed.

20

JEB SMITH AND LUKE Suttle were keeping watch up by the wagons, though it was still early enough in the night that some of the folks had not turned in.

Zeke and Marie sat by the dying embers of their campfire. Their son, Daniel, was asleep under the wagon. Caleb Driscoll was there with them, too, still awake. Caleb had just returned from a conversation with Captain Walker. Most of the recent evenings, when supper was finished and the camp was settling in, Caleb would wander over to Captain Walker's wagon where the veteran would share stories of fighting the Indians in Florida. Most of his stories had little to do with Indians and more to do with swamps and alligators. Caleb had never seen an alligator and had trouble conjuring one in his mind. But he was fascinated by the stories.

Elias and Madeline and their children were over at Jason Winter's wagon with Jason and Maggie. Maggie being their oldest daughter, they were more comfortable relying on her for provisions than anyone else in the wagon train.

But for the most part, the camp had settled into a quiet attitude. Many people were already asleep.

Zeke recounted for Marie how he had saved a little of their money.

"I knew if Rimmer told Elias a hundred dollars a piece he'd told his outfit something less than that and intended to put the remainder in his own pocket," Zeke said. "He'd told them fifty a piece. He intended to take an extra two hundred and fifty for himself."

"He's a vile man," Marie said. "All of them are."

"He reminds me of those men we encountered at South Pass. Hubbard and his outfit. I suppose the wilderness draws a man of a certain sort."

"I don't think that's true," Marie said. "It drew you and your brother. It drew Reverend Marsh and Captain Walker and all these other men."

Zeke was about to offer a response when a shout over near the livestock caught his attention.

"What's this about?" Zeke said.

They had a couple of campfires burning, but Zeke couldn't see much of anything at first. Just some shadows of cattle or horses. But then one of the campfires started to grow, like it had jumped into the sagebrush. And there was more shouting now. And beyond the shouting, Zeke could hear the cattle begin to low. Something was disturbing them. Towser and Mustard were both over beside Daniel, curled up under the wagon, but Towser came out first, fully alert. In the dying light of his own campfire, Zeke could see the dog's tense body and perked ears. Then Towser started to run, and Mustard followed behind him, both dogs barking. Zeke recognized Towser's bark. Something was bad wrong over where the livestock grazed.

"Indians," Zeke breathed. "Get Daniel, get inside the ring of wagons."

And then a rifle shot rang through the night. Zeke saw the sparks fly from the rifle, orange in the black night. It looked like the gun was shot into the air. And then he heard the unmistakable sound of a stampede. A rumble of hooves on earth. And the fire was spreading quickly, now lighting up the scene so that Zeke could see the shapes of cattle beginning to run.

"What's going on?" someone shouted.

"It's a stampede!" someone else shouted.

The camp around the wagons broke into chaos. Men and women were shouting everywhere. Women were calling for their children. Men were barking orders, mostly shouting at each other to arm themselves. The fear of Indian attack spread rapidly.

Down among the livestock, there was more shooting. Two shots followed that first one. Then another. The cattle were in a full stampede, and it sounded to Zeke like some of the horses might be running, too.

And then Elias was beside him, his Leman rifle in his hand and his Colt saddle gun holstered on his hip.

"What the hell is going on?" Elias said.

"Indians scattering the stock?" Zeke suggested.

The dogs were barking, and their barks were getting distant. That meant they were chasing cows and the cows were still running. Towser was a herder by nature, and it wouldn't have surprised Zeke to see that dog come back nipping at the heels of a dozen cows. Mustard was a retriever, and a good hunting dog, but he wasn't a cow dog. The best he would do is drag back a cow's rear leg if he could wrench the thing loose.

"Who have we got down there with the livestock?" Elias said.

"I think Henry Blair is there. Will Page. Maybe Billy Tucker, too."

"Who's shooting those guns?" Elias asked.

"I couldn't say, Elias."

"I guess we'd better go and have a look," Elias said.

They weren't alone. Several of the emigrants owned livestock – spare oxen, horses, steers, or some just had a single milk cow. Anyone who now feared the loss of their property was making their way over to where the livestock had been gathered for the night.

The fire was growing, and before starting over to the livestock, Zeke grabbed a tin pot. He filled it from his water barrel and then poured the water over a quilt, drenching it. Caleb joined them, and the three of them moved at a quick pace. The livestock were being held for the night about a hundred yards from the wagons. The oxen for the wagons and a few horses were held inside the circled wagons to keep them from wandering. That way they could quickly be hitched to the wagons and there would be no delay in moving out in the morning.

Though Elias already realized there would be a delay.

"Keep your eyes open for Indian raiders," Elias cautioned Caleb and Zeke, though they'd seen no sign of Indians at all.

Here and there, a man ran past, a rifle in his hand. Depending on who it was, Zeke or Elias might shout a word of warning. A man might trip and fall and accidentally shoot his neighbor in the dark. Most of the murders on the trail happened accidentally, they knew, and many of these rifles were tetchy things, and accidental discharge was just about as common as sagebrush.

Fortunately, the sagebrush in this particular spot was common but not dense. Caleb took one corner of the wet quilt and Zeke took the other, and they laid it down over the burning sagebrush and stomped it out. The quilt was ruined, but the fire wouldn't spread.

Elias gave the fire a kick and fed it with some sticks and some brush that was sitting nearby, and in a moment it was burning bright and casting light in their immediate vicinity.

Henry Blair came riding up the moment he saw Elias.

"Mr. Townes! We've got a helluva problem. We've got cattle scattering every direction."

"I see it, Henry," Elias said. "What happened?"

"It was Mr. Rimmer," Henry said. "Him and a couple of them others, they started slapping cows and horses and then starting waving burning logs at them. They stampeded them on purpose."

There were still horses and cows that hadn't run, milling about and grazing.

A T FIRST LIGHT, EVERY man who could sit a horse and rope a cow was in his saddle, unless his horse was among those that ran off, and then he was on foot.

"We've got to round up as many of these critters as we can as fast as we can," Elias said. "And then we've got to get the wagon train rolling."

A search was made through the night for Rimmer and his men, but Elias and the others quickly determined that they'd been abandoned by their hired guides.

"They got me to pay them extortion money and then they ran out," Elias said.

"More than just that," Solomon McKinney said. "I'm missing sixty dollars from my wagon."

When he heard that Rimmer and his men had absconded, Solomon's first instinct was to light a lantern and search his wagon. Like Zeke, he'd taken the measure of the men and he had a bad feeling. A quick search revealed his wallet of money was missing. Others then searched their own wagons, and through the night, several people realized they'd been robbed. Most of them were missing forty or fifty dollars. Some were missing more.

"Who can say how long they've been stealing from us?" Wiser McKinney said. "They certainly didn't do this all yesterday. They've probably been robbing us since we left Fort Hall."

"Why send off the cattle?" Walter Brown asked. "It was an unnecessary insult after the injury."

"They did that to be sure we didn't try to follow them and get our money back," Solomon McKinney said. "They'll make their escape while we try to roundup our livestock."

"Talking about it don't help nothing now," Elias grumbled. "Now we've got one thing to do. We've got to roundup the livestock. Every man who doesn't have a horse needs to get a rope and start walking. Most of the animals ran north. You men with horses, we'll ride out and round up whatever we can find. Everyone should be back here by noontime, and we'll roll out with whatever we've got."

The men split up, some walking and some riding out farther. The mounted men passed many horses and cattle in those first couple of miles, which boded well. There was a good chance the cattle hadn't stampeded too far and they would be able to regain most of their herd.

Elias rode with Zeke and Henry Blair. The Tuckers and the Page brothers and Jerry Bennett and Jeff Pilcher all rode with them, as well. Zeke's dogs, Towser and Mustard had come along. Towser did lead three cows back during the night, a feat which Zeke boasted in throughout the morning.

"He's a damn good dog," Zeke told Elias. "If we had time enough, I'd just sit back at camp and wait for him to bring all of them in."

Even when they were about five miles from camp, they rode past cattle grazing on the prairie. They figured it would be better to find those farthest away and turn them back, picking up strays along the way, than trying to gather a cow here and there and bring them back.

"We're lucky that it seems they gave out before they got too far," Elias commented at one point.

They rode maybe six miles, climbing up onto high hills and checking into low spots whenever they came across them, and finally they stopped seeing scattered livestock.

"Let's turn back here," Elias said to the others.

They fanned out, remembering the places where they'd seen cattle. They were easily covering a swath two to three miles wide. Within a half hour of turning back, they'd already collected two horses and eight steers and were driving them back.

Zeke had just dropped down into a dry wash where he found a couple of cows grazing on some grass. He waved his coiled rope and called to the cows and got them moving up out of the dry wash, and that's when he heard a shot from some distance.

"Ha!" Zeke shouted at the cows, urging them forward. "Get up there!"

As soon as he cleared the rim of the dry wash, Zeke looked around for confirmation that he'd heard a gunshot in the distance. But he didn't need confirmation from the others. At that moment, he heard a string of shots – six or eight shots.

The men were spread out considerably, a hundred yards or more separating one man from the next, but they were within sight of each other. Each of them was looking around at the others, trying to get a sense of what to do.

Zeke pushed the cows ahead of him, zigzagging Duke behind them, and when he'd pushed them out thirty or forty yards and had them moving in the right direction, he wheeled Duke and galloped toward Elias.

"That shooting's back toward the wagons," Elias said.

"Yeah. No question about that. Maybe some of the others trying to push livestock?"

"I hope to hell not," Elias said. "They'll just start another stampede."

"Somebody saw a snake? Walter Brown's shooting at his boots again?"

Elias shook his head.

"That's Henry out yonder that way," Elias said, nodding his head. "Whyn't you ride out to Henry, tell him to pass the word to the others to keep on with the roundup. You and I will ride back to see what's happening with that shooting."

Zeke dragged reins and started at a lope out to Henry. Elias didn't wait for him, trotting off in the direction of the wagons and waving his hat to try to drive the cattle he'd collected out toward the others.

Zeke had to go at a hard lope to catch up to Elias, and the two of them kept that pace to get back to the wagons as fast as possible.

As they neared the wagons, there could be no mistake that something was amiss. For one thing, there were cattle spread all out over the place and no one driving them back, even within a couple of miles of the wagons. The men on foot, who'd lost their saddle horses in the stampede or never had a horse to begin with, they should have been out here bringing this livestock in.

But as they got nearer, the evidence of some catastrophe was even greater.

Several men were walking to the west some distance from the wagons, all of them toting rifles. It looked as if they'd formed up a small militia and were marching off to battle. As soon as Elias and Zeke came into sight, some of the men started waving frantically at them.

Both men broke into a gallop.

The first thing Zeke saw was Marie's face as she and Maddie and some others came out to meet Elias and Zeke. He also noted up near the wagons a man on the ground with several people tending to him, as if he was hurt. Zeke couldn't see who it was.

21

"It was Rimmer and three of his men," Madeline Townes explained to her husband. Tears streamed down her face, and she was frantic when Elias and Zeke rode up. Elias dropped down from the saddle and took her by the shoulders.

"Calm down and tell me what happened," Elias said to her.

"I saw them coming, and I thought it was some of our people," Madeline said. "I didn't think anything of it. They were walking their horses, calm as you please."

"About the time we realized it was Rimmer, that's when they charged," Marie added. "They were armed with rifles. Mr. Long went out to greet them. He was also armed with a rifle. They shot Mr. Long."

Long was one of the packers in the party. His horse had been spared from the stampede because his horse was inside the perimeter of the circled wagons overnight, but Elias decided the packers should rest their animals rather than be a part of the roundup. He also had it in his mind that if Indians should attack the wagon train, those men would be there to protect the women and children. But he never considered that Rimmer would come back.

Madeline was breathing now, getting herself under control, though her cheeks were still wet with tears and her eyes red.

"They took Maggie," Madeline said.

Elias swallowed hard.

"Our Maggie?" Elias said, and he gave Maddie a shake of the shoulders. "My daughter?"

"Yes," Madeline said.

"And two other girls," Marie said. "They took one of Mr. Brown's daughters. And Sophie Bloom."

Elias had gone pale, and Zeke could see the rage building inside of him. Elias the planner. Looking around now, his hands still gripping Madeline's shoulders, counting out his advantages and disadvantages, forming a plan in his mind for saving his daughter.

"Jason rode after them with Captain Walker and Gabriel and Christian," Maddie said.

"What are those men doing?" Elias said, looking at the small band of volunteer infantry toting their rifles and marching out across the prairie. It was every man left at the wagons, and only a handful at that.

"They're going after them," Marie said.

"Damn fools," Elias said. "They need to come back now. Protect the livestock and property."

Elias shook his head in dismay. A gang of poorly armed, untrained farmers and merchants – on foot! – pursuing five bad men on horses.

"Let's ride," Zeke said. "Ain't but five of them. We need to catch Rimmer before Jason and the boys get themselves killed."

Elias clenched his jaw and gave Zeke a hard look.

"I'm going with the intention to kill all of them," Elias said. "Just so you know before you get in the saddle."

"Yep. That's what we're riding to do."

Both men stepped back into their saddles. Elias went at a trot out past the men marching, but Zeke reined up and spoke to them.

"Captain Walker and some others rode after them on the horses we still had," Luke Suttle said. "The rest of us are going to try to catch them on foot."

Zeke shook his head.

"You men go back to the wagons," he said. "Protect your wives and your daughters. Protect the property and the livestock. Me and Elias are going to get the women back."

"They took my daughter!" Walter Brown said.

"And we're going to get her back," Zeke said. "You men help the others that are bringing back the livestock. Keep your rifles close to you. And when the livestock are back, you camp one more night. In the morning, you start moving along the with the Snake River. We'll catch up to you."

"You want us to leave you?" Luke Suttle said.

"I want you to keep this wagon train moving. We need to get the livestock to better forage and better water, or we'll all be lost."

Zeke didn't stay to argue. He gave the reins a tug and let Duke go to catch up to Elias.

"They scattered the livestock so that we'd leave the women defenseless," Elias said.

"I think that's right," Zeke said. "Last night and this morning, I thought they did it so we wouldn't chase after them. But now I think that's what they did. They probably spent the night not far from us."

"They're heading west to those mountains," Elias said.

"How do you know that?"

"Rimmer all but told me. Said he'd hunted and trapped in those mountains. Said there's good water and forage there."

They'd ridden at a lope over some distance, but now had the horses walking to save them. The ground was broken and hilly in front of them as it neared the mountains off in the distance. At times, they'd ride into a low spot and not even see the mountains. In the high spots, they'd search the horizon for Rimmer and his men or Captain Walker and Elias's sons, but after more than an hour of riding, they still hadn't seen them. But they knew they were behind them.

In the sand, they could see the tracks of the horses, both Rimmer and his group and the horses belonging to those men led by Captain Walker. It looked, in fact, like Walker had deliberately kept his tracks from intermingling with Rimmer's tracks.

An hour grew to two, and Elias and Zeke were again at a lope. The mountains in the distance were growing larger, filling the horizon. They reached into the foothills now, and the change in terrain was evident. The sandy ground was replaced by a rockier earth. More grass filled in those spaces between the dusty sage. There were still no trees to speak of, but they could see now that the sides of the mountains were covered in what they guessed were western red cedars and pines.

Two hours became four. The sun was beyond the mountains, not set, but no longer visible in the sky. Already the temperatures were beginning to drop in the shadow of the mountains.

The hills here made for deep ravines, and following the tracks was becoming more difficult. In the low spaces where water flowed in creeks during the spring, cedar trees and scrub oak grew. Up on the high spots, pinyon and juniper dotted the hills in between large outcroppings of basalt.

Elias and Zeke lost their certainty that they were following in the wake of Rimmer and his men. Now they had to rely on a broken branch or a spark on a rock that proved riders had recently come through this way.

Elias had gone some time without saying anything, and Zeke knew what was weighing on him. Rimmer and those others, they knew these mountains – at least a little bit. They had planned their escape and predicted pursuit. Those men were surely confident that they could lose themselves and hide in these mountains. And Elias was beginning to lose hope.

"We're going to find them," Zeke said.

"I don't know how they left us so far behind," Elias said. "They had at least a couple of mules when they left out last night."

"Maddie said it was Rimmer and three others. One of them probably came on ahead through the night while the others camped near us and waited to attack the wagons."

"Probably so," Elias nodded. "They had this thing planned out. They were probably planning it for days."

"Probably planning it ever since we left Bridger's Fort," Zeke said.

"I should have known better than to hire them," Elias said. "I brought this on us."

"You didn't know they would turn out to be like this. How could you?"

"They are unsavory men. I could see that at a glance."

"Most everyone you encounter out here is going to be unsavory," Zeke said. "They got no laws of conduct and no civility. Almost anything they encounter in this countryside is trying to kill them. It's enough to turn a man unsavory. Rimmer and his men are worse than unsavory, though. They're putrid, rotten to their cores. Give me all your unsavory men, the hard men who are disagreeable, and I'll tame this country. But Rimmer? He's putrefied flesh. He's what we need the unsavory men for. And before that sun finishes setting, you and I are going to be unsavory."

Elias nodded his head.

"Let's go and find him," Elias said.

But their search would not last long.

They rode down a draw and up over a ridge, and it was up on that ridge where they heard a rifle shot nearby.

A CREEK RAN DOWN through the canyon below the ridge, clear as glass. Perched in his saddle up on top of that ridge and looking down at the creek, Elias could almost taste the cool and clean water. That stream curled its way down from the ridge opposite where Elias sat. The bottom of the hollow was covered in cedars and scrub oaks, enough cover that Elias couldn't see anyone. Of course, the hollow was also shrouded in shade now that the sun had dipped below the far mountains.

"Better drop down out of that saddle," Zeke said, keeping his voice low and taking his own advice. He tied Duke to the branch of a cedar and slid his rifle free of its scabbard. He pulled a paper cartridge from his cartridge box on his belt and rammed it home. "I'll put a cap on it when we know what we're shooting at."

Elias, too, dropped from his saddle and loaded his rifle.

They'd heard the one shot, and it sounded like it had come from down in the hollow. But even now as they went over the side of the ridge and started down the hill, they saw nothing in the hollow. The hillside went steeper in spots, and they had to descend it with their feet perpendicular, a hand out to stable them against the incline. Rocks slid under their feet.

A cedar root exposed from the ground like the handle on a trunk allowed Zeke to grab hold with one hand and swing himself down a vertical drop of about four feet. He stepped out of the way, and Elias jumped down, too.

"You see anything?" Zeke said.

"I do not," Elias said.

Then another shot burst, and down in the canyon it echoed, making it hard to locate even the direction from which it had come.

"Up this way?" Elias said, pointing his rifle upstream of the little creek flowing through the canyon.

"Sure," Zeke said, though his tone gave Elias to know that he wasn't sure at all.

They reached the canyon bed and started making their way now deeper into the canyon, moving among the thick juniper and red cedar.

"All this time we've spent on the open prairie, not a tree in sight, I feel a mite closed in," Zeke said.

And then Elias saw movement up ahead. He held out a hand to stop Zeke, and pointed. Up ahead, half hidden in the shadows and behind the trees, they could see several horses. Elias sidestepped several feet to get a different look, and then he waved Zeke forward.

"It's Christian down there, holding the horses."

Now the two men hurried forward, and when they were still some distance away, Elias called out in a hushed voice.

"Chris! Hey, Chris!"

The boy jumped like a spooked horse and spun around, but his eyes fell immediately on his father and the relief was plain to see.

"Pa! They've got Maggie," Chris said.

"We know, son. What's going on here?"

"We followed them into this canyon," Chris said, and he pointed down toward the mouth of the canyon. "They dismounted up ahead there, and they're backed up against some rocks. Captain Walker told me to lead the horses back here to keep them safe."

Elias nodded his head.

"Tie them off so they don't run if the shooting gets thick," he said. "We're going up with the others."

Zeke could see them, now. About twenty yards ahead of where Chris stood with the horses, Zeke could see several figures squatting down behind basalt boulders or hugging the bark of cedars. He recognized Captain

Walker peering around the side of a cedar, and Jason Winter, pressed tight against another tree. There was his nephew Gabriel crouched low behind some rocks.

Maddie had only named the four of them – Walker, Jason, Gabe, and Chris – but Zeke saw two others. Paddy O'Donnell, an Irishman who was packing to Oregon City, and Mike Corder who was packing only as far as the Wascopam Mission.

Elias called ahead to let them know he and Zeke were coming up on them. Both men crouched low and made their way over to where Captain Walker pressed himself against the cedar.

"They've shot at us a couple of times," Captain Walker said. "We're hunkered down here. We can't shoot back because they've got the women."

"Where are they?" Elias asked.

Captain Walker looked around the tree again, and then he came back behind the cedar.

"You see that big outcropping of rock? They're down behind that. They turned their horses loose a little deeper down into the canyon. I think there must be one of them farther back with their animal, and just four of them there at the rocks."

"The women are with them there at the rocks?" Elias asked.

"Yes, definitely," Captain Walker said.

"Do you have any thoughts?" Elias asked.

"We have better options now that the two of you are here," Walker said. "Perhaps a flanking maneuver that would put the two of you in behind them? If you could work up and over that ridge, perhaps follow the creek down."

Elias nodded his head.

"I was thinking along those same lines."

"Whatever we do, Mr. Townes, we should do it soon. If we let it get dark and they still have the women in their custody, I fear we'll never see them again."

Elias glanced at Zeke.

"What do you think?"

"Up and over the ridge," Zeke said.

The canyon made a sharp turn in the space between Walker's contingent and Rimmer's men. That turn would allow Elias and Zeke to climb the ridge without being seen. Then they could move along the ridge and, as Captain Walker suggested, follow the creek back down.

"Don't shoot on them," Elias said. "Don't risk hitting one of the women."

22

ELIAS HANDED HIS RIFLE to Zeke and then squeezed himself into the crevice. To reach the top of the ridge, they had to scale a vertical cliff. Only ten or maybe fifteen feet, but tall enough to make it a chore.

Inside the narrow crevice, Elias wedged his back against one side and his feet on the other. He shimmied up a couple of feet like that until he could reach a ledge. Then he dragged himself up, finding crannies where he could step and push himself until he was up on the ledge.

"Hand me up them rifles, then come on up here," Elias said.

Zeke fed him the rifles one at a time. The ledge was narrow, but long, giving him plenty of room to lay the rifles down and then step back so that Zeke could drag himself up the same way Elias came.

With Zeke giving him a boost, Elias was able to get his fingers over the top rim of the cliff. Now he dragged himself up and Zeke put his hand under one of Elias's feet to steady him. With some grunts and curses, Elias managed to clear the rim.

"Gonna be tougher for you," he told Zeke as his brother handed up first one rifle and then the other.

"I'll manage," Zeke said.

He was younger and more agile. They were both big men, but Zeke wasn't carrying as much weight to try to drag over the top. He found a couple of narrow spots where he could get a toe in and, even without the best hold, managed to get up close enough to the top that Elias could get a hand around his wrist. Then, together, they got Zeke up to the top.

They crouched down to avoid being seen and started making their way along the ridgeline to get in behind Rimmer and his men.

The back of the canyon rose in a long draw, the little spring-fed creek sliding through it from somewhere well above the canyon rim.

Even in the moment, Elias felt a momentary envy at the water. What he wouldn't give to be able to bring their livestock to drink and their water barrels to refill from that creek.

"Let's work our way down to the draw, get at them from that way," Elias said.

They moved at a jog, backs hunched and rifles held low to try to keep their profile smaller, less noticeable.

But as they moved, they heard a sudden volley from down below. Four rifles barking out almost simultaneously. Elias and Zeke paused to see the cloud of white smoke drifting out from behind the basalt outcropping where Rimmer and his men had sought cover, the gunsmoke cutting through the cedar and juniper.

And now they were on the move. Neither Zeke nor Elias had a clear view of it, but they could see movements of dark shapes in among the canopy and the deep shadows.

"They're trying to make their escape," Zeke said.

"We've got to cut them off in the draw," Elias said.

He could envision it now. Elias and Zeke would be the surprise Rimmer hadn't expected – especially behind them on the draw.

"They'll come mounted," Elias thought out loud. "If we don't stop them from getting past us, we'll never catch them."

"We'll stop them," Zeke said.

"We can't shoot," Elias said. "We can't risk the women."

"We'll figure it out."

Zeke's confidence – it had kept him alive when he found himself alone for four or five hundred miles through the South Pass. It had kept his family alive when they fell under attack from Hadden's men with Zeke alone to save them. Zeke's confidence was in part where Elias drew his own confidence to journey to the Northwest Territory in the first place.

Their jog now became a run, as much as they could run hunched over.

There was shouting down below now. Elias figured Captain Walker and the others were aware that Rimmer and his men were moving. Surely, they would press on them, push them back.

They'd reached the creek and started to follow it down through the draw. The cover here at the top of the draw was less. Not as many cedars. The junipers were sparse and skinny. Both men moved behind the brush and trees as best they could to keep out of sight.

First came Loop Garoo, a halfbreed Indian whose father was French-Canadian. He led a string of two mules packed with provisions. He was well in front of the others, and Elias guessed he'd been the one who came into the mountains by himself overnight and hadn't been there when Rimmer and the others rode into camp to steal the women.

Both Elias and Zeke ducked down behind a juniper.

"Hold this," Zeke said, and he leaned his rifle toward Elias. Then Zeke began pushing caps down over the nipples on his saddle gun.

"What are you doing?"

But there was no time for Zeke to answer. Garoo was nearly on top of them now.

Zeke stepped out from behind the juniper and raised the Colt revolver, drawing back the hammer as he did to release the trigger.

Garoo's eyes grew wide at Zeke's sudden appearance, and he couldn't even pull the horse wide.

Zeke pulled the trigger and dropped the hammer on the saddle gun. It spit out a cloud of gray smoke and spark. The gun barrel so close it was nearly pressed against Garoo's side when it exploded. Garoo let loose a yelp as the punch of the bullet knocked him clear of his saddle. The horse and mules kept lunging up through the draw, but Loop Garoo was on the ground now, grunting and holding his side. It was a grievous wound in his side, pouring blood through his fingers.

The shot had surely alerted the others in Rimmer's outfit to danger ahead, but Zeke could hear the horses coming on.

"Rifle!" Zeke called to Elias, holstering his saddle gun and holding out his hands.

Elias tossed the rifle to Zeke and then stepped out on the other side of the juniper.

Henry Temple emerged from the shadows of the trees, mounted on a big sorrel with Sophie Bloom lying across the saddle in front of him. She was kicking her legs wildly and shouting, and Temple had the reins in one hand and the other hand held her dress, twisted into a knot for him to hold onto, and pressing her down into the saddle.

Elias shouldered his rifle.

"Stop!" he shouted at Temple. "Stop or I'll kill you!"

A wide grin spread across Temple's face and he leaned forward a touch. The big sorrel took the slope of the draw in bounds, heaving itself forelegs and back. Temple made for an enticing target. With Sophie laid across the saddle the way she was, Elias had a clear shot.

Elias squeezed the trigger.

From the short distance, he couldn't miss.

Sophie Bloom screamed.

Henry Temple took the shot directly in his neck. He shouted once, and the hand that held Sophie Bloom's dress shot to his neck. Elias had just a glimpse of blood coming between Temple's fingers, and then Sophie Bloom was in the air, thrown clear by the horse or by Temple or both.

Temple's sorrel dashed past Elias, and Elias made no effort to stop him. He dropped the rifle to the ground and reached for Sophie.

Bowdon came now, just him in the saddle. And the man Duhon came just on his heels.

Zeke leveled his rifle at Bowdon, seeing the man didn't have a captive, took his aim, and squeezed the trigger. But Bowdon's horse was coming at a gallop, and Bowdon hugged the horse's neck. The shot flew high, into the cedar trees beyond Bowdon, and now Bowdon rolled himself out of the saddle, landed on his feet and was immediately in a run, coming for Zeke with a long knife in his grip.

Zeke flipped his rifle around, intending to use it as a club, but Bowdon was within reach already. He grabbed the butt of the rifle and gave it a jerk, pulling Zeke off his balance. He stepped in and swung the knife, opening a vicious gash across Zeke's left shoulder.

Zeke gritted his teeth against the pain and staggered back. Bowdon yelled a visceral, blood thirty shout. Seeing his prey injured, Bowdon pounced.

The rifle was gone and Zeke had no tool with which to defend himself. He threw up his arm and felt the knife slice him to the bone.

Duhon had Walter Brown's daughter in his saddle with him, and he'd been trying to get through right behind Bowdon. But the moment Bowdon dropped down from the saddle, the big sorrel bucked and stopped, blocking Duhon's way. He had to rein up.

The girl was straddling the saddle, sitting up in front of Duhon. He had an arm wrapped around her waist to prevent her from going anywhere, but she prevented him from having good control over the horse. The animal was skittish and irascible, and as Duhon tried to wheel the horse and take the slope from a different angle, the horse declined to cooperate.

The confusion with the horse allowed Elias to get close to Duhon, without even being seen. He tossed his rifle aside and drew the saddle gun, cocking back the hammer and releasing the trigger.

Elias didn't dare shoot with the girl pressed against him. He knew a bullet could pass right through a man. So he kept the gun down, dashed in at the side of the horse where Duhon wouldn't see him. He jumped up and grabbed the man by the collar and jerked him backward, using his own weight to drag Duhon over.

And then it was all three of them – Elias, Duhon, and the Brown girl – on the ground. Struggling. Elias wrapped his arm around Duhon's neck, holding the man from behind, and the Brown girl managed to wriggle free.

Sophie Bloom had recovered from her fall. She was sore and shaken, but mostly unhurt. She rushed over to Walter Brown's daughter, wrapped her arms around the girl and pulled her back, out of the way.

Duhon used his elbows, jabbing them at Elias. Most of his blows fell wide or were spent as Duhon twisted to get around at Elias, but a couple of them connected painfully. Elias swung the saddle gun around and bashed Duhon in the face with it, right across the bridge of the nose. Duhon's hands flew to his face, and Elias pushed him off now. Elias rolled, putting a knee into Duhon's back, and he pressed the saddle gun against the back of the man's head.

It felt like a callous dispatching of a man's life, but Elias gave nothing more than a passing thought to it. He swung now, seeing Bowdon slashing his knife at Zeke. Elias's brother was a bloody mess. Blood across his arm and face and chest.

Elias thumbed back the hammer on the saddle gun and leveled it at Bowdon's back. He squeezed the trigger, but the hammer fell on a dud cap.

Elias cursed the gun and dashed forward now, raising the Colt into the air above his head. He brought it down with all the force he could muster, and the heavy barrel smashed across Bowdon's head, opening a gash and staggering the man.

Zeke was on the ground, squeezing his left arm close to his body to try to hug away the pain of the gash on his shoulder. But his right hand found the grip of the knife on his belt. Bowdon wobbled on his feet. Zeke thrust the knife up, cutting open Bowdon's belly so thoroughly that both men knew immediately it would prove to be a fatal cut.

But Elias never gave it the chance.

He cocked back the hammer, rotating the cylinder and put the barrel of his saddle gun against Bowdon's head. That shot was instantly lethal.

Neil Rimmer watched the others charge through the combatants ahead.

He had no idea who was up there, or how many, or how they came to be there. But he could hear the other men pursuing behind him, making their way up the draw.

"We're only going to have the one moment to escape," Rimmer whispered into Maggie Winter's hair. "You do anything to foul up my getting through there, and I'll shove this knife so deep into your side you'll see it come out the other end. You hear me?"

Maggie whimpered her response.

She could feel the blade of the knife he held at her side pressing into her. She could feel the stinging where it had already cut her slightly. She could feel the sticky blood. She was pressed against the man, stuck between him and his saddle horn.

"I killed that Barnes girl," Rimmer confessed. "You understand what I'm saying to you? I took that girl, I killed her, and I took her scalp as a souvenir. I won't think twice about digging your innards right out of you."

Rimmer sat his horse, waiting. He'd not seen Garoo go through, but he'd heard the shot and knew its implication. Garroo was dead, or nearly so.

Temple had broken free. He'd lost the girl, but he'd gotten through. In what state, Rimmer couldn't be sure. Maybe he'd gotten through as a dead man. Rimmer was fairly sure the shot fired at him had struck its target.

Bowdon was a fighter, and Rimmer edged the horse forward – while staying in the shadows – to watch Bowdon fight. Duhon got caught. He might have made it through if he'd been smarter about going in behind Bowdon.

Rimmer started to go when he saw the man drag Duhon from his horse. Was that Elias Townes? Maybe. Rimmer couldn't see clearly enough to know for sure. If it was, Townes had done well to catch up to them.

When the man shot Duhon, Rimmer knew this was it for him. He'd have to go now, or he'd never make it. Bowdon was still fighting, probably about to win his fight, but now it was going to be two against one.

"Hold on little gal," Rimmer said.

The reins were loose on the horse's head, tucked in between Rimmer and the girl. He had his knife at her side and his other hand gripped her by the arm, holding her in place.

"Ha!" he shouted, and gave the horse a jab in the sides with both heels.

The horse bounded forward. Stretching and reaching to get up the slope. They dashed out of the shadows just as Elias Townes shot Bowdon in the back of his head.

Rimmer saw Townes turn fast, bringing up the saddle gun. But Townes only just had a glimpse of the horse and riders.

"Daddy!" the girl shouted in the space of that glimpse.

In just a moment, Rimmer and the girl were clear. The horse thrusting them higher up the slope, out of the canyon.

Somewhere along the way, maybe a hundred yards or so beyond where the fighting took place, they passed by Henry Temple's horse and the two mules. Temple was on the ground on his back, his eyes staring lifeless at the sky above. He had a nasty wound at his neck. It looked like half his neck had been shot away.

Rimmer had no idea where he'd go, but he knew his opportunity to get away lay in the darkness. He just had to last another hour.

They went higher, breaking out of the canyon and following the ridge as it snaked up a long mountain spur.

The ridge overlooked the creek which ran about twenty feet below. It was rocky, uneven terrain, and they'd not gone far when the horse stumbled and kicked rocks.

Rimmer reined up, grumbled some. He squeezed Maggie hard by the arm so that she squealed, and then he flung her from the saddle. She landed on her stomach, the breath knocked out of her. Rimmer dropped down from the saddle beside her and gave her a kick.

"The horse is spent," Rimmer said. "We're walking now. You're going to get up and you're going to walk with me. If you try to run, I'll cut your neck open. If you try to get away, I'll cut your neck open. If you don't do exactly what I tell you to do exactly when I tell you, I'm going to cut your neck open."

He grabbed her and jerked her bodily to her feet and slapped her across the back of the head. He liked abusing her because he knew it would keep her compliant.

He pushed Maggie ahead of him and led the horse. He couldn't abandon the horse. He would need it to get out of the mountains and back to Bridger's.

Up ahead, he saw a high rocky outcropping sitting like a turret on top of the ridge. It actually protruded out, over the hill, big enough that there might be space to hide. But he wouldn't have to worry about anybody getting around behind him there among those rocks.

"Make for them rocks up there," Rimmer said.

23

ELIAS HAD TO RUN to catch the sorrel horse. He'd gone for it once, but the horse trotted away from him. When he finally caught it, the horse eyed him nervously. Elias talked to the horse, put a hand on its neck.

"You're going to be okay," Elias said, trying to strike a balance between the urgency he felt and the need to keep the horse calm long enough for him to get in the saddle.

He gave the horse a gentle pat on the neck, stepped into the stirrup and hoisted himself up into the saddle. Now he rubbed the sorrel's neck.

"You're all right," he said, taking up the reins. "Now, let's go."

Elias left Zeke without a word. He didn't give a second look to Sophie Bloom and the Brown girl. They would figure it out. Captain Walker was making his way up the draw and would be there soon enough. Elias just knew he had to move quickly before he lost Rimmer and Maggie in the dark.

They'd gone fast and were out of sight when Elias cleared the rim and found the natural path of the ridgeline. But he had no doubt that Rimmer had come this way. Any other way would have turned him back to danger.

He passed Henry Temple's dead body and spared a thought for Reverend Marsh and his wife. Knowing what he knew now, Elias figured Reverend Marsh was murdered. He might never know the truth – probably never would know.

Elias kept the sorrel moving up the ridge, his eyes moving constantly, left and right, seeking any sign of which way they might have come.

"Rimmer!" Elias shouted, and his shout echoed back at him from the canyon walls below. "Turn my daughter loose, and I'll let you live!"

No response other than the echo of his own voice came to him. Elias urged the sorrel along the ridge.

Up ahead he could see a large, rocky outcropping. Almost circular. It jutted out over the hillside below. It looked like a straight drop of maybe fifteen feet or more, and then a severe drop along the rock-scattered face of the hillside. The slope dropped maybe another sixty feet or so before it crashed into the canyon bottom below. The outcropping was big enough that a man and a woman might find a place to hide there, and perfect for making an ambush. Elias reached down to his holster and drew out the saddle gun. One chamber of the five in the cylinder was empty so that as he rode there would not be an accidental discharge. He'd fired two rounds out of it and had a misfire with a third chamber. He had one shot left.

Elias clicked his tongue at the sorrel.

The horse climbed along the ridge, nearer to the rocks. And then Elias saw the horse tied to a juniper at the bottom of the rocky outcropping. That was it. Rimmer had come to this place and stopped his flight. Tying the horse at the bottom of the rocks, he'd clearly not come here to hide. He'd come here to make a stand.

Elias dropped down from the saddle, held his gun casually in front of him, and edged around the rocky outcropping, looking in all the crevices and behind the boulders for any sign of Maggie or Rimmer.

Near the top of the rocks, Rimmer pushed Maggie into view from out of a crevice. He held a knife at her side and stood behind her where Elias wouldn't have a clear shot at him.

"Why don't you toss that hand cannon on the ground there," Rimmer said.

"Let her go and I'll let you live through the night," Elias said.

Rimmer scoffed. They were in deep shadow, and Elias just now noticed the stain on Maggie's dress right where Rimmer held the point of the knife that looked like blood.

"Are you hurt?" Elias asked his daughter.

"No. Just scared."

Elias nodded his head.

"Mr. Rimmer's going to see reason here, Maggie," Elias said. "He's going to let you go in just a moment."

"Small chance of that," Rimmer grinned.

"Turn her loose and you can take your horse and ride out of here," Elias said. "If you do anything else, this ends with me killing you."

"That's some bold confidence, Mr. Townes. Maybe it ends with me killing you."

"It won't," Elias said. "You're fighting for your life, and I expect you'll put up a helluva fight. But I'm fighting for my daughter, and I promise if you don't give her up now you're going to find that you don't have what it takes to beat me."

"This is a wild country, Mr. Townes. A man only survives on what he can win with his hands. And the man who survives takes what he wants. You understand me? The only law in this country is right here in your own two hands." To emphasize his words, Rimmer held out left hand, palm up and fingers flexed. "I am the survivor, Townes. Me. When people like you need help, it's to people like me that they turn. I am the survivor. I am the law in this land. I take what I want, and no man can stop me."

"No law in this land?" Elias snarled at the man. "Maybe not. Maybe not before. But it's changing, Rimmer, and you've underestimated men like me. Men like me are bringing a new law with us. It's the law of right and wrong. Men like me are going to tame this country. And we're going to take it away from men like you."

Rimmer chuckled and shook his head.

"You couldn't do it, Townes. You ain't strong enough. You ain't a survivor. Ain't no way men like you can ever take anything from men like me. But if you want it, that's the only way you're going to get it. You'll have to take it, 'cause we ain't gonna give it up."

"You've misjudged me, Rimmer. I'm a family man, and that girl there is my family."

Rimmer scoffed, grinning his grin. The light was fading fast, now. Elias knew he had to end this now. If darkness caught them, anything could happen.

"Put down that hand cannon if you don't want to see your daughter's innards," Rimmer said.

Up in the rocks, Rimmer was probably ten or fifteen feet higher than Elias standing down on the ridge. Elias had no shot with the gun, not with Maggie standing in front of Rimmer. He had no advantage.

He thumbed down the hammer on the saddle gun and set down in the dirt at his feet.

"That's the way," Rimmer said. "Now step on that horse and ride back down the ridge."

Elias glanced at the horse, and when he did, he saw Jason Winter, Captain Walker, and Gabriel making their way up the ridgeline, mounted on their horses. They were coming at walk, easing their way to avoid being seen by Rimmer.

"I'm not going anywhere until you turn her loose," Elias said.

Rimmer laughed.

"How about I turn her loose over the back of these rocks?"

The motion was swift, almost flawless. Rimmer spun Maggie to his side so that she was facing the back side of the rocks, and then he gave her an almighty shove. Maggie screamed as she fell headlong toward the back of the rocky outcropping.

As soon as she was gone, Rimmer jumped from the rocks, pouncing like a mountain lion going for its prey.

THEY'D SEEN ELIAS FROM down the ridge a ways, but they couldn't see Rimmer or Maggie. They were hidden in the shadows and the rocks.

Jason Winter was out in front. His leg ached to no end. Back at the South Pass, he'd had his horse shot under him, his leg smashed by the horse. He'd been weeks healing and still suffered with a limp and pain when he rode. It had made the journey since Bridger's Fort excruciating for him.

But when Rimmer and his men rode in and stole Maggie and the other girls, Jason didn't give another thought to his leg. And now he rode out front of Captain Walker's posse. Desperate and in a rage. More than anything, Jason Winter wanted to kill the man who stole his wife.

"They must be in those rocks," Captain Walker said. "Elias is talking to someone there. Everyone just stay calm. Let Elias handle it."

But then they saw Elias set down his saddle gun, and even Gabriel said, "What's he doing?"

And then Rimmer and Maggie stepped out away from the rocks, just enough that they were out of the deep shadow. Jason could see his wife now, and his instinct was to bring the horse to a gallop, to race forward and save her.

"Just be calm," Captain Walker said. "Mr. Townes knows we're here."

Then, Jason saw his wife go flailing toward the back of the rocks.

"Maggie!" he shouted.

Rimmer flung himself off the rocks, crashing bodily into Elias Townes.

Jason Winter gave his horse a slap with the loose reins and the horse started at a gallop. He watched in horror as Maggie dangled from the rocks for a moment, struggling to hang on, and then fell. She dropped with a scream fifteen feet to the steep, near-vertical, hillside below. This hill was covered in loose rock, and several big rocks broke free when Maggie fell, clattering down the steep incline. Maggie slid another ten feet or so, finally coming to a stop when she grabbed the branch of a pinyon pine clinging to the hill.

Captain Walker and Gabriel both broke into a gallop, too, following behind Jason.

Elias was on the ground, knocked half senseless when Rimmer jumped on him and knocked him over. Elias rolled away as Rimmer swung the knife wildly, and then he was on his feet.

Rimmer swung the knife in a big arc, and then swung it back. If he'd noticed the three riders, he showed no sign of it. His back was to them. His eyes were fixed on Elias. Jason reached the outcropping first, and he swung his leg over the side of his horse. He ran to the precipice and found Maggie about twenty feet below, maybe more.

"Hang on, Maggie!" Jason shouted.

He turned back toward his horse and grabbed his coiled lariat. He tossed it down over the side. Maggie was lying against the slope. One foot had found a rock protruding from the ground, and she stood against that while holding to the pinyon branch with both hands.

"Put the loop over your shoulders," Jason called to his wife. Careful not to let go of the branch, Maggie worked the loop over her shoulders and around her body so that it was snug under her armpits. Jason turned to secure the loop to his saddle horn so that he could use the horse's strength to pull her up.

The fight still raged behind him.

Captain Walker charged forward like he was back in Florida fighting the Seminoles. In his hand he clutched his old cavalry sword, raised high above his head.

Only now, hearing the horse thundering toward him, did Rimmer take his eyes off Elias. He turned just as Captain Walker reached him. Walker swung the cavalry sword down at Rimmer, slashing the man across the face and shoulder.

Rimmer twisted and fell back.

Now Elias had a chance. He grabbed Rimmer's wrist in both hands and turned it violently. Rimmer's knife fell away, and Elias began raining blows at the man's head. He drew up a knee, crashing it into Rimmer's guts, and Rimmer fell onto the ground. Elias spun, searching for his gun. He found it in Gabriel's hands. His son had dismounted behind Walker and grabbed the gun.

Gabe had the hammer back, the heavy gun in both hands pointing at Rimmer.

"Do it, boy!" Rimmer shouted with a laugh, blood streaming from his nose, his face cut and dirty. "You ain't got the stones!"

Gabe closed his eyes and squeezed the trigger. The hammer fell. Rimmer winced and drew back. But either the cap was another dud or it had been knocked off. There was no percussion.

"Ha!" Rimmer shouted and he started to laugh. "I didn't think you had the stones, but you didn't have the powder!"

Elias jerked the knife from his own belt and plunged it into the man's chest.

24

PADDY O'DONNELL AND MIKE Corder got a fire going before dark.

Zeke sent Christian Townes up to the ridge to get Tuckee and Duke.

Captain Walker and Gabriel rounded up the horses and mules that Rimmer and his outfit had brought with them into the mountains. They made a camp down in the canyon bottom near the clear stream.

Sophie Bloom went through the packs on the mules and found a couple of shirts that she tore into bandages. She dressed Zeke's wounds as best she could. The knife wound on his arm being the worst.

From Rimmer's supplies, they found beans and bacon for supper, but they spent a cold and sleepless night there in the canyon. No one suggested burying the bodies. Without any mention of it at all, they'd all agreed that the coyotes could have them.

The women, whose fate had seemed so dark for so many hours, didn't mind the cold or the meager provisions.

In the morning's light, Elias went through the saddlebags and the packs. He found hundreds of dollars in money stolen from the emigrants. They took the mules and the horses and rode out of the mountains. They didn't move fast. Zeke was hurt bad, between his shoulder and his arm. Elias and Maggie both felt the aftermath of the rough treatment they'd endured. When at last they arrived near the Snake River, they found the place where the others of the Townes Party had camped for the night.

221

"They've gone on," Elias said, though no one needed him to say it.

The campsite was abandoned. The only trace of them were several burned out campfires and the tracks of the wagons.

"I told them to go on," Zeke said. "As we rode out yesterday, I told them to keep the wagons moving."

"They haven't all gone," Mike Corder said, riding his horse a ways from the camp to a mound of rocks, at the head of which stood a cross made from two branches from a cottonwood tied together with twine.

"That'll be Mr. Long," Paddy O'Donnell said. "I guess that shot he took yesterday killed him."

The eight men and three women kept moving on through the afternoon. Late in the day, they saw the circled wagons up ahead of them.

Madeline Townes had the most to be thankful for when she saw her husband returning with her oldest daughter and her two sons. She ran out to meet them. Maggie climbed down from her horse for her mother's embrace, but Maddie had to drag both Gabe and Christian from their saddles.

Walter Brown could not stop expressing his gratitude to Elias for bringing back his daughter.

Sophie Bloom, pregnant and now without a husband, had only her mother and children to come out to greet her. But Cody Page waited for her, and when she'd spent time with her mother and her children, he went to her.

"I'm sorry I wasn't there yesterday when those men came and took you," he said to her. "I took on the chore of driving your wagon, and I know that don't mean I have all the responsibilities. But if I'd have been there, I'd have protected you."

"You're very sweet to say so, Mr. Page. But no apology is necessary. You were doing what you needed to be doing."

She looked rough and ill used. Her face smudged with dirt. Her arms scratched and bruised.

"Is the baby okay, Miss Sophie?" Cody asked.

She nodded her head.

"I believe so, Mr. Page."

Marie Townes took her husband back to their wagon. She cleaned and dressed his wounds. He winced and pulled away as she tried to clean the slash to his arm.

Captain Walker spent the afternoon and evening sharing the story of the rescue of the three women with all who cared to hear. When the sun had set and the cook fires were dwindling, he found himself at Elias's wagon.

Elias was eager to turn in for the evening. Exhausted, and he felt the weight of the coming morning pressing on him. It would be up to him now to get them back on the trail. It would be up to him now to figure out how to get the Townes Party over the Blue Mountains where they were all but certain to encounter snow. How could they survive the snow and get beyond the mountains? When would they finally arrive at the Columbia River? Would it be too late in the season to build rafts and float to Oregon City?

He just wanted to sleep and face the questions in the morning.

But Captain Walker was feeling elated after his brief return to battle, and he wanted to commune with his fellow combatants.

"I've talked to a fair number of our fellow travelers, Mr. Townes, and I can report to you that no one is sorry at the loss of Mr. Rimmer and his men."

"I suppose not," Elias said.

"Though there are many now who are worried about how we will move forward without a proper guide."

"If it's consolation to them," Elias said, "you may tell them that Rimmer never was a proper guide."

Captain Walker chuckled.

"I suppose he was not," Walker said. "But the concerns are legitimate, all the same."

"We'll get there," Elias said. "It's just moving people and wagons and livestock from one place to another. We've come fifteen hundred miles together. They can trust me to get them the last five hundred."

"Yes, of course," Captain Walker said. "But you understand the worry?"

"I understand the worry," Elias said.

Madeline had been scrubbing a pan, but now she came over to sit next to her husband near the dying embers of the campfire.

"Captain Walker, you can tell anyone who is worried that if they think they can do better on their own then they are welcome to try," Maddie said. She put a hand on Elias's shoulder. "For my part, I happily trust myself and my children to the man who has proved himself capable over and over again on this journey."

"Yes, ma'am," Captain Walker agreed, and he stood up now and brushed off his britches. "Nobody doubts Mr. Townes' competence. But we're coming into the worst part of the trail – the most unbroken part, I mean. And we all know how late it is in the season. And with no experienced guide, people are afraid."

"They needn't be," Madeline answered him.

Dear Reader,

Thank you so much for riding along with Elias and Zeke and the rest of the Townes Party on the Emigrant Trail.

I sincerely hope you've enjoyed the first two books in this series.

Elias Townes has led his wagon train nearly to the confluence of the Boise River and the Snake River. Fifteen hundred miles of the Oregon Trail's two thousand miles are behind them. But the hardest miles are still ahead.

It's late in the season and the Townes Party is sure to face snow in the Blue Mountains.

But worse may be waiting for them when the get out of the Blues. Will it be too late in the season to even finish their journey and reach Oregon City?

With the hardest miles still in front of them, they may face **Tragedy on the Barlow Road** before they can reach their destination.

I hope you'll click the link and grab your copy of the third book in the **Townes Party on the Oregon Trail series: Tragedy on the Barlow Road**.

Sincerely,

Robert Peecher

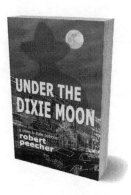

If you enjoy crime thrillers, I'd be grateful if you would check out my Barnett Lowery series beginning with "Under the Dixie Moon."

It's deep-fried Southern justice when an investigator returns to his small town roots to take on a corrupt sheriff and the Dixie Mafia. If you love stories of down-home murder up in the hills of Dixie, small-town criminals, and deep-fried Southern justice, then slide into the passenger seat of this '67 Camaro and buckle up. You might want to bring along your Colt Python, because what gets buried Under the Dixie Moon always comes back up.

Click here to grab a copy today!

If you love traditional Westerns, I'd encourage you to check out my Robert Peecher author page on Amazon.

If you've never read any of my Westerns before but you're interested, I would encourage you to take a look at these books:

"Too Long the Winter" – a short, standalone novel that's a great example of my Westerns.

"Bred in the Bone" – The first book in the Heck & Early series.

"Rankin's Posse" – The first book in the Marshal from Ocate Trilogy.

"Blood on the Mountain" – The first book in the Moses Calhoun Trilogy.

All of these and more can be found on the Robert Peecher author page on Amazon.

Robert Peecher is the author of more than 60 novels. He's an avid outdoorsman and loves paddling rivers and hiking trails. He lives in Georgia with his wife Jean. You can follow him on Facebook at Robert Peecher Author.

Made in United States
Troutdale, OR
11/24/2024

25138229R00142